Ready for Anything

THOMAS WAUGH

First published in 2017 by Endeavour Press.

This edition published in 2018 by Sharpe Books.

ISBN: 9781793044808

"I simply love you more than I love life itself."
Elton John, *I Guess That's Why They Call It The Blues.*

"No human being can really understand another, and no one can arrange another's happiness."
Graham Greene, *The Heart of the Matter.*

READY FOR ANYTHING

1.

London. Bermondsey Square. Pistol shots cut through the balmy, evening air and shattered the party atmosphere. The muzzle flashes and sounds were all but simultaneous, as when thunderclaps follow lightning. The flats, hotel and bars, which formed two sides of the square, trapped and amplified the terrifying noise.

Run. Hide. Tell.

Those were the three words of advice, issued by the authorities, should the public become embroiled in a terrorist attack.

Pint and highball glasses crashed to the ground. Chairs and tables were knocked over. Screams spiralled upwards like tendrils of smoke from chimney stacks. Flip-flops slapped against paving stones. Fearing further gunshots, or a nail bomb, or a savage knife crime, the late-night revellers ran for their lives – scattering like a colony of insects under attack.

It was every man for himself. A stampede. More than one woman was pushed over and trampled upon. One twenty-something, wearing a beany hat and ripped jeans, was more concerned with holding his phone aloft and filming the scene, than helping the girl he floored get back on her feet. He would spend the rest of the evening tweeting about the attack, desperately trying to play the victim (or even hero) in a campaign to glean more likes and followers on his social media accounts. Maybe his ex-girlfriend would get in touch, to see if his was okay, he reasoned. He emailed *The Guardian* to say he was available for comment, enclosing two profile pictures from his Facebook account. In one he was duly solemn, but in the other he was smiling and holding his thumbs up. It had been taken in Australia during his gap year, just before he was about to bungee jump. For half an hour or so his hashtag, #iwillsurvive, even started trending. It was the most exciting moment of the software developer's life.

The stream of people continued to flow out of the square and into Tower Bridge Rd. Traffic screeched to a halt. Hands trembled – and voices broke – as all manner of young professionals called the police. Panic was pandemic. Tears cut through make-up, like scars.

Run. Hide. Tell.

It was a terrorist attack, they fervently believed. A few witnesses reported that they had heard the perpetrators exclaim, "Allahu Akbar."

But one man swam against the stream. The forty-something had been standing, alone, in a corner of the square, keeping himself to himself. Michael Devlin looked anonymous. A no one. He was dressed in unbranded jeans, a polo shirt and sports jacket. Few had given him a second look but some might have thought the man was waiting around for someone. Others might have imagined that someone had just left him. He was drinking. Brooding. Contempt smouldered off him like brimstone, albeit one couldn't quite tell if the contempt was directed towards himself or the surrounding snowflakes. Most likely it was both. The more Devlin thought about humanity, the more he loved his dog.

Devlin still cradled his tumbler of Bushmills as he walked towards *Shortwave* – a cinema and bar – where the shots emanated from. The former paratrooper, having served in Afghanistan, was no stranger to muzzle flashes. As a former contract killer Devlin could also tell the difference between a gangland hit and Islamist terrorist attack. He sucked in the scene as he walked, making a risk assessment and noting the entrances, exits and CCTV cameras.

His red-rimmed eyes narrowed, as he peered over the sea of bobbing heads to take in the gunman and his confederate, standing by their two victims. A cold moon shone down, indifferent to the crime.

The two corpses looked similar. Brothers, perhaps. Eastern European. Probably Albanian. Devlin had heard a rumour they were aggressively moving into the area, peddling drugs and trafficking and young girls. Both victims had shaved heads. Both wore designer tracksuits and diamond-studded earrings. Tattoos decorated their necks – a spider's web and crucifix. The bullets had thudded into their broad chests. They were slumped in their chairs, heads lolling to the sides, as if sleeping. Even when they appeared at peace however in death the two men were unpleasant looking and their thuggish faces betrayed their brutal hearts. Scallop-sized pieces of flesh were strewn on the ground behind them, from the bullets having entered and exited their bodies.

A whiff of cordite stained the air. Devlin breathed in the smell, like the familiar and moreish aroma of cigarette smoke. His hand yearned to grip his Sig Sauer pistol. His trigger finger even made a couple of subtle, reflex pulling motions. But the weapon was now at the bottom of the Thames. Devlin had tossed the pistol after his last hit, when he had accidentally gunned down a friend.

The wiry Jamaican gunman, Isaac "Shanks" Ridley, wore an expression of confoundment more than anger as he noticed Devlin standing a dozen paces or so away from him. His face was thin, greasy, cadaverous. A grin, or grimace, revealed a crooked gold tooth and receding plum-coloured gums. A dusting of grey around his temples coloured his otherwise black hair. The rest of the square was now deserted. The wind whistled eerily through it, like a small town in the old west. His bloodshot eyes were stapled wide-open, with cocaine and sadism. The money was good – his boss would pay him well for the hit, after the Albanians had put one of their crew in the hospital – but money wasn't everything. Ridley enjoyed violence, like some people enjoy wine, computer games or mountaineering. Back in Jamaica he had used a cutthroat razor, whilst making his name as a young enforcer. Violence was visceral, thrilling. He still carried a blade but times had changed. He could have fun with guns too, and there was no need to wash your hands or buy a new shirt after each job. Ridley savoured the sense of power, just before and after pulling the trigger. He relished the look of unadulterated fear in his victim's eyes. His expression would contort in pleasure in direct contrast to the contortions of terror and misery he witnessed – or rather inspired.

Devlin drained the rest of his drink. The whisky warmed his throat and stirred his heart. As well as there being a sense of defiance in his features, he also seemed to be wryly half-smiling at his fellow hitman. Because he knew something his counterpart didn't.

Ridley made a sucking noise through his teeth and the smile turned into a vicious sneer. He shook his head at Devlin, to convey how he thought the drunk was either transgressing or acting dumbly. The white boy should have run. He should have hidden. There are no more heroes left in the world. Innocents had been injured – or killed – in the crossfire during previous jobs. Ridley would still sleep easy at night if he murdered the foolhardy stranger. And he would do it quickly. The police would be on their way and he wanted to get back to his boss' cellar bar in New Cross. Rum, spliffs and girls would be waiting for him there, as well as a plane ticket to a non-extradition island, just in case the hit generated too much heat.

The yardie raised his gun but Devlin didn't flinch, either from fearlessness or fatalism. The stoical contract killer had stared down the barrel of a gun before – one that was loaded too. Instead of hearing the report of a Browning handgun being fired Ridley just registered a click. He even pulled the trigger again, in hope or desperation.

It was now Devlin's turn to shake his head. The gunman was transgressing and acting stupidly at the same time.

Amateur.

Devlin proceeded to walk towards the Jamaican, as if he were a new recruit again, purposefully marching across the parade ground at Aldershot. Ridley let out a curse and reached into his pocket for a spare magazine but as he did so Devlin's empty tumbler glass struck him square in the chest. Ridley was forced backwards and he dropped the gun and magazine. In the meantime, Devlin picked up a glass ashtray from a nearby table, where gobbets of Albanian blood marked various tapas dishes and a jug of sangria. Just as Ridley gazed up and regained his focus he felt the white boy grab him by his shirt and gold chain - and glimpsed the ashtray being thrust towards him. The first blow smashed into his front teeth and knocked him unconscious. Ridley fell to the floor, like a ragdoll. Devlin's expression remained calmly determined, or impassive, as he bent over his opponent and drove the ashtray into his face two more times, as if his arm were a jackhammer. Bone glinted beneath the gashes in the yardie's nose, cheek and chin. The brutal attack lasted just a few moments. Devlin neither knew – nor cared – if the figure at his feet was dead. Adrenaline began to course through Devlin's body but he still had the presence of mind to place the ashtray in his pocket. He'd retrieve the tumbler too. He didn't want to leave any trace evidence.

Ridley's young confederate, Justin Gardner, took in the sudden change of events, his mouth agape. It was the first time the teenager had taken part in a hit. Tonight was supposed to be another test. He still needed to prove himself. Earn the respect of his fellow gang members. Ridley instructed that there was no need for the youth to carry a gun.

"Just watch and learn, young cub," the older man said, with a mischievous and menacing gleam infusing his doped-up expression.

Drugs had yet to ravage Justin's features, or dull the teenager's aspect. But he believed his path was set. He could make more money in a month than his father had made in a year, before he left. After tonight he could put a down payment on the car he wanted – and get his girlfriend the lingerie she (or rather he) picked out on the *Victoria's Secret* website. He would order the latest iphone and only wear designer labels. But the money wasn't just for himself, he vowed. He wanted to buy his mum a new flat, in a better neighbourhood, and send his younger brother to a better school. But first he would get the keys to the Mitsubishi Evo. Justin had dreamed about the car, ever since he first played Grand Theft Auto when he was eight.

Devlin quickly, professionally, loaded the gun and levelled the weapon at the petrified teenager. The hit wasn't supposed to turn out this way, for Justin. It felt like a dream. Or nightmare. His bottom lip trembled and his soul eked out an inelegant prayer. Whilst Ridley was being savagely, or clinically, assaulted by the stranger the young gangster had pulled out a blade from his inside coat pocket. He had threatened to cut someone before, but had never actually bloodied the weapon. Gardner stood at the crossroads, caught between fight or flight. Beads of sweat wended their way along his down-filled cheeks.

"You've brought a knife to a gunfight," Devlin drily remarked. "Go. Or if you're going to come at me, come at me now."

Police sirens sounded in the background. At any one time forty vehicles, containing armed officers, patrolled the streets of London – ready to respond to violent crimes and terrorist attacks. The aim was for the authorities to reach any possible scene within eight minutes.

Part of Devlin wanted the youth to attack him, stab him. He was ready to die. *Nothing is good or bad but thinking makes it so.* He deserved to die. Life weighed upon his chest like a tombstone. He wanted to die, as much as a bridegroom desired his bride on their wedding night. Devlin had sinned, more than he had been sinned against. Guilt scythed through him like a bolt of lightning, every day... And the widower would only be able to see his wife, Holly, in the next life. Not in this one.

The teenager's heart skipped a beat but then galloped. His breathing became irregular – and there was a moment when he nearly lost control of his bowels - but somehow Justin began to shuffle backwards. Self-preservation was sovereign over any loyalty he felt towards his confederate. His eyes flitted between the coal-black pistol and the stranger's flinty aspect. Justin resisted the temptation to turn around, out of fear of being shot in the back, but retreated into the bar. Spilled kettle chips and cashew nuts crunched beneath his feet. The speakers still piped out acid jazz. Once he made it to the kitchen door Justin ran – and didn't look back. Cutlery and crockery crashed to the floor. He dreaded breathlessly explaining events to the getaway driver, parked close-by on Long Lane. He further dreaded having to explain events to Onslow, his unforgiving boss, waiting for him back at the bar – *The Rum Punch* - in New Cross.

Devlin slipped the Browning into his jacket pocket. He would dispose of the weapon in the Thames.

The police sirens grew louder. Wailing. Out of the corner of his eye he could see a few curtains, in apartment and hotel windows, peel back a little. But no one secured a good look at the man who hadn't run or hid.

Devlin calmly, unassumingly, left the square. Head bowed down. His hands buried in his pockets. Most people were too glued to their smart phones to notice him. Devlin already had his route home planned-out, one which avoided any CCTV cameras.

The moon disappeared behind some thick grey clouds, congealing across the sky like a scab. Police cars began to light up the scene, like a disco, in the background. But Devlin didn't look back as he tabbed down a poorly lit side street and the night swallowed him up.

2.

Devlin threw the gun in the river. The Thames gratefully gulped it down. He now lay curled up, in a foetal position, on his sofa. A large brandy sat on the coffee table in front of him, as did a full ashtray and well-thumbed copy of Bernard Malamud's *The Assistant*. He closed his eyes and exhaled. His conscience smarted not from having injured, or killed, the recidivist in the square. He was pleased however for having spared the trembling adolescent. He was young, but not innocent. *There are no innocents left in the world.* If nothing else, the lapsed Catholic believed in original sin. Devlin believed in God too. He just couldn't serve Him.

The curtain rhythmically billowed out, as if someone were standing on the balcony with a set of bellows. Warm air – and the abrasive sound of police cars gunning down Tower Bridge Rd – entered the room. Devlin reached over for the remote control and turned down the volume on the stereo. *The Bob Dylan Playlist* was on, again:

"*Most of the time*
I'm clear focused all around
Most of the time
I can keep both feet on the ground
I can follow the path
I can read the sign
Stay right with it when the road unwinds
I can handle whatever
I stumble upon
I don't even notice she's gone
Most of the time."

Devlin thought how it was almost a year to the day since his last hit. The target had been Rameen Jamal. The Afghan, who had murdered and maimed his friends during a routine patrol of a village in Helmand, had been staying at *The Ritz*. Devlin had arranged, through the fixer Oliver Porter, to have the cameras hacked and temporarily disabled at the hotel. As well as Jamal, Devlin also assassinated Faisal Ahmadi that night. Ahmadi was travelling in Jamal's diplomatic party. He was a person of interest for MI6, for his involvement with various Islamist terrorist organisations.

But not all had gone to plan. Devlin was unaware that his former commanding officer, Charles Tyerman, was serving on the Afghani's security detail. He unwittingly shot the man who, a few days before, offered him a job. A future. Afterwards Devlin told himself that Tyerman should not have elected to work for Jamal (even though it could have been the case that his ex-CO was there that night under the auspices of the intelligence services, to keep watch over the Afghanis). Devlin had to shoot his final target in the hotel suite quickly, else he would have been shot himself. He didn't know it was Tyerman, before he fired. He told himself it wasn't his fault. *But there are no innocents left in the world.*

After the hit a year ago, in the dead of night, Devlin had gone for a walk and sat upon a bench, by the shimmering Thames. Police sirens echoed out in the night then too. Devlin promised himself that, should somehow the authorities come for him, he wouldn't run and he wouldn't hide. He also wouldn't tell, in regards to giving up Oliver Porter in return for a shorter sentence.

It was also nearly a year to the day when Emma walked out on him. If he would have asked her to stay she may have changed her mind. But he didn't. The end came after Devlin cancelled their trip to Paris. Emma had nurtured a hope that the man she loved would propose there. But she asked the question: does he love me? The inconvenient truth was that Devlin was still in love with his late wife, Holly. He still visited her grave every week, played her favourite songs, stared at her picture and re-read old letters. Devlin still had one foot in the past. Or rather one foot in her grave. Tears streaked down Emma's face, of despair and anger, as she confessed how she felt. She wanted to hurt him – and said a number of things she later regretted. Her throat became sore. Whilst Devlin remained calm. Or cold. He understood how she felt and it was indeed best that they end things, he remarked. His tone was laced with more relief than regret, which only made Emma despair – and grow angrier – all the more.

There were times when Devlin missed Emma – and was tempted to get in touch to apologise to her. Try to make amends somehow. Atone. But what good would it have done? She had found someone else and he would still ultimately keep his promise to Holly, never to re-marry or fall in love again.

It was almost six months to the day, when his foster-mum, Mary, passed away. Cancer ploughed through her body like a plague of locusts and death came three months after diagnosis. Devlin made the funeral arrangements and gave the eulogy. Before she died Mary made her son promise that he would regularly visit his foster-dad in the care home. The couple had been married for over fifty years. Devlin tried to visit every few days, but Bob Woodward's condition grew worse after his wife's death – and lately he barely recognised his foster child. Tragically Bob often forgot that his wife had passed away and he would ask Devlin where she was - and break down on hearing the news, as though he were being told for the first time.

Devlin would take his wheel-chair bound father out into the care home garden for a cigarette and navy rum. His mind and body were diminishing by the week, curling up on themselves like an old, mouldy slipper. Moments of lucidity were rare, precious and increasingly infrequent, like a sunny day in March or October. Everything is born to die. The inevitable truth provides little consolation however. Bob Woodward's skin was stretched over his face like parchment. His grey hair was now snow white. Liver spots flared up on the back of his hands and temples, like daffodils blooming in spring. His foster-dad's once wide, toothy grin had grown narrower, or had disappeared altogether. Devlin's father was sinking further into the black hole of vascular dementia and there was nothing he could do about it. He felt guilty on the days when he didn't visit the widower – and depressed on the days he did.

Violet, who had been laying on the floor by Devlin, suddenly got up. She padded into the kitchen and then came back again, gazing at her master expectantly. The black and white mongrel had a sweet temper, expressive face and lively manner. Somehow, she had the power to pull Devlin out of his own black hole, when it began to suck him in. He got up from the sofa, walked past the bin in the kitchen, overflowing with bottles of vodka and takeaway cartons, and filled-up her water bowl. Perhaps Emma knew how much Devlin needed Violet, which was why, in one last act of love, she let him keep her after they separated. It broke her heart, but it would have broken his more. Devlin stared down at the mongrel, a former stray. Small beads of water dripped from her chin. Her tail wagged, cutting through the fog of his listlessness. For the first time that day the former soldier managed the semblance of a smile. It was a weak smile, but a smile nevertheless.

"*I can survive and I can endure*
And I don't even think about her
Most of the time."

3.

Oliver Porter stood in his parlour and sampled a glass of the Claret he decanted earlier in the evening. Moonlight washed over a manicured lawn as he peered out through his conservatory window – and caught his own reflection as he did so. He had lost weight and kept it off, he thought to himself, gently pleased. Not even his bitterest enemies, of which the former fixer might have owned a few, could call him "paunchy" now. His doctor said that his blood pressure was "sterling" – and he no longer needed to be proscribed statins.

Porter was wearing a camel-coloured summer suit from Chester Barrie and a crisp, white Huntsman shirt. Not a hair, black or steel grey, was out of place on his head. The former Guards officer had regained a little more of his military bearing and gait since regaining his figure. A tan, gleaned from a recent family holiday in the Seychelles, gifted him a further air of vitality and happiness. Partly he had ventured to the island paradise to go sea fishing. The middle-aged conservative suddenly had an appetite to try out new things. He had started writing a novel, about a wily diplomat serving the Byzantine Emperor Alexios Komnenus during the First Crusade. Porter was also learning to tie his own flies and every Friday night he took pleasure in cooking a three-course meal for his family. Retirement was not the hell he once thought it might be. Few things perturbed Porter. Fly-fishing taught him the virtues of patience and stillness. If he had lost his head, as an officer or fixer, then others would have lost theirs. Being "passionate" was vulgar. The Englishman believed in retaining his sangfroid, even when he didn't feel like doing so. It was good for business and his soul.

The furniture was somewhat eclectic in the room, but things still worked and played off each other. His wife had been responsible for furnishing most of the house. Her excellent taste was the least of her admirable qualities however. Victoria was waiting for him upstairs. The children were away for a few days, staying with friends. She had asked him not to be too late in coming up to bed. The fixer didn't need a cryptologist from MI5 to decode what she meant.

Porter emitted a contented sigh and smiled. A number of investments he'd made a decade ago had just matured. Money makes money. His children were performing well at school and thankfully reading outside their narrow curriculums. He recalled his son's laughter last night, when Porter had told him a joke whilst they put away his air rifle:

"Margaret Thatcher, Tony Blair and Jeremy Corbyn are all standing in a line. You have a gun but only two bullets – and your mission is to save the country. What do you do?... You shoot Jeremy Corbyn, twice."

The precocious boy laughed and then cheekily replied:

"I'd need to watch that the bullets don't go straight through, as there's nothing between his ears."

Porter's smile widened as he glanced at the newspaper on the arm of his wingback leather armchair. Derek Hewson, the Tory MP for Cheltenham, had resigned from office – and Porter hadn't even needed to fix the welcome outcome. Porter had been hired by Hewson and a group of lobbyist a couple of years ago. A freelance journalist was about to sell a story - concerning the politician having sent lewd photographs, via text messages, to underage girls. Porter bribed the journalist – and arranged to put him on staff at a major newspaper – in return for burying the story. When he returned home that evening, having fixed things, Porter found it difficult to look his wife and daughter in the eye. He's leapt, before he's been pushed, Porter thought to himself. He imagined the sleazy MP, standing before the party chairman, wringing his hands and trying to worm his way out of things. In the article, the dutiful politician claimed that he wanted to spend more time with his family. Knowing how much his wife rightly despised him though, Hewson was at least starting to receive his just desserts, Porter idly thought.

He wrinkled his nose briefly, deliberating on whether to smoke a cigar or not. He had cut down on his smoking and drinking over the past year or so, but Porter was still far from puritanical in his habits. Ultimately though he resisted the temptation. There was mettle more attractive upstairs and he didn't want his breath smelling of smoke when he made love to his wife.

It had been their wedding anniversary a week ago. Porter took Victoria to the same restaurant, near Warminster, where he proposed.

"As much as I admire you Oliver for having given up certain things in your diet, which you used to harp on about not being able to live without of course, the thing I most appreciate is that you have given up your work for me and the children. We're all enjoying your retirement."

Victoria had never asked too many questions concerning her husband's work. Perhaps she knew the truth would frighten or appal her. He called himself a consultant, which wasn't altogether a lie. But Oliver had spent over a decade consulting on ways to launder money, ruin reputations, cover-up scandals and even assassinate people. When his life – and that of his family – had been put in danger by some particularly unsavoury clients – the Parker brothers – Porter decided that it was time to untie the Gordian Knot and extricate himself from his profession. He had saved himself. But Devlin had saved him too, having gunned the gangsters down before they could get to Porter and his family.

Devlin. His former associate was an old photograph he would take out of the draw every now and then. Sepia-tinged. Devlin was the most honourable man Porter knew – and the most tragic. The two things were linked. His vow to his late wife, never to marry again, had condemned him to a life of loneliness (albeit one could preside over a harem and still be lonely, Porter conceded). Through keeping his promise to one friend in Afghanistan – and assassinating Rameen Jamal – Devin had ended up killing another.

The two men had attempted to keep in touch after their last job together. Porter invited Devlin to lunch at *White's* but his guest turned up drunk and they largely sat in silence. A fortnight later Porter invited Devlin to stay over at his house for the weekend. But something was missing. Perhaps the two men reminded each other of their previous lives, which they would have preferred to forget. Victoria noticed the change in her husband's friend immediately:

"He's there but he's not there... Is he on some form of medication? He's like some burned out candle or empty shell case... Michael looks older as well. You can tell he's been drinking... The children seem wary of him too, where they used to find him fun and fascinating."

After that weekend Porter determined not to contact Devlin again, unless he contacted him first. The fixer had come out of retirement for the assassin once, to help with the Afghani hit. But the first time would be the last. His debt had been paid. Honour had been served. He was not his brother's keeper, Porter declared to himself.

Devlin was just waiting around to die now, although one could have argued that we are all guilty of that. But Devlin was ready to die – and not just in a spiritual sense. He had already purchased the suit he wanted to be buried in. His plot was picked out too, one close to his wife's grave. He just needed someone's permission to end things, it seemed. Was he waiting for a sign? Perhaps from his God, Porter mused.

Just before Porter was about to head upstairs his phone rang. *Unknown number.* He was tempted to ignore the call, but it might have been one of the parents his children were staying with for the weekend.

"Hello," he remarked. If the word was expressed as a question as much as a greeting then Porter didn't like the answer.

"Hello, old boy. It's the ghost of Christmas past, Mason Talbot, here. I apologise for calling you at such a late hour. I hope I've not disturbed you and your good lady wife, Victoria."

His skin prickled and a chill slithered down Porter's spine as he heard the CIA operative's voice. Especially when he casually – but deliberately – mentioned his wife's name. She had never met the American, not did Porter ever want her to.

"No, it's fine," Porter replied. Polite, but far from warm.

"I was wondering if you would be free for lunch tomorrow? And I won't take no for an answer."

Talbot's tone was collegiate, charming. Faux English. But beneath the civilised veneer of the agent from New Hampshire there resided a black, serpentine soul. Talbot came from what passed as aristocratic stock, for America. Old family money, originally earned from molasses and later oil, had paid for the finest education at Yale and Oxford. Talbot's father, a priapic Democrat congressman, had then used his influence to grant his son an entrée into the world of military intelligence. Mason Talbot did possess an official job title, although no one quite knew what it was, but more so he worked in the shadows – a law unto himself. The senior CIA operative, who had recently celebrated his forty-ninth birthday, had been stationed in London for over a decade. He oversaw, or instigated, black-ops in Britain and the rest of Europe. Talbot also ran assets and gathered intelligence, with or without the cooperation of MI5 and MI6. Although the American was not beyond sharing information with his allies, he always made sure he received more than he traded away. "As with when I convert my currency, I like a favourable exchange rate," he would smoothly remark.

In some regards Porter regarded his American cousin as a fellow fixer. Just a more powerful and menacing one. The two men had several meetings and meals together, around five years ago. Talbot had offered the Englishman a stipend, with the promise of further payments to follow, should Porter be able to provide him with poignant intelligence on his clients.

"Think of yourself as becoming a professional gossip. We are both aware that you work in the service of various people of influence, whether it be in the worlds of commerce or politics. I would just like you to be paid twice for your labours. I would like to know what you know, or who you know... I like you Oliver. We are cut from the same cloth.

Indeed, we even share the same tailor do we not? As Thatcher once said of Gorbachev, we can do business together."

Porter had no intention of being drawn into the American's web and politely declined the offer to become one of his assets. It had been over three years since he had even spoken or seen the CIA agent. Wariness – or fear – eclipsed a sense of curiosity as to why he was getting in contact again. Talbot was one of the most dishonourable – and dangerous – men Porter had ever met. He pictured the man behind the convivial voice on the end of the phone. His slim, almost feminine, jawline and cleft chin. His blond hair, which he probably now dyed. His turquoise eyes, bright and yet cold at the same time. Bleached teeth. Handmade shoes. His gold signet ring, bearing his family crest, which he often stared at – as he assessed whether he needed another manicure or not. Talbot could smile, re-fill your class and fraternally clasp your hand – right up to the point, or after, of sheathing a knife in your back. Even his compatriots spoke ill of him, albeit they only did so when whispering. Mason Talbot was akin to an unctuous villain from an unfinished Eric Ambler novel.

Porter noted down Talbot's precise instructions, after agreeing to meet the American for lunch. His skin prickled again when he mentioned Devlin's name in passing. Porter firmly pressed "call end" on his phone, hoping that if he pressed it hard enough he might never hear from Talbot again. The smile on his lips had fallen, shattered, like a piece of fine porcelain dropping to the floor. He sighed, wearily. To help settle his stomach Porter poured himself something stronger than wine. He gave some thought as to why the American would contact him, accessing a rolodex in his mind of reasons as to why their paths should now cross. The scene outside darkened, as the moon seemed rinsed of light. Brittle. Porter eventually trudged upstairs. The stairs - or his bones - creaked. His shoulders seemed more rounded. His head was bowed down in prayer or logical thought. The husband would apologise to his wife. He would explain that he was tired, or had a headache. But the last thing Porter felt like doing right now was making love.

THOMAS WAUGH

4.

There was no CCTV footage of any suspects, regarding the incident in Bermondsey Square, the authorities lamented. Eyewitness reports were contradictory. The photofit of the man the police were looking for resembled a Slavic Jason Statham. Ridley had been put into an induced coma in order stabilise his condition. It was unlikely the gangster could, or would, aid enquiries once he recovered. If he recovered. As disturbing as the crime was however there was a general mood of relief that it was not another terrorist attack. The gangland killings would soon be yesterday's news.

God is smiling on me, Devlin ironically mused as he turned off the television. As he readied himself to go out he glanced at a framed print on the wall, of Anton Mauve's *A Dutch Road*. The picture was a replacement for one that Emma had taken with her when she moved out. After surveying the artwork, he glanced in the mirror (if the picture wasn't already a mirror to his soul). His eyes narrowed, or face winced, as took in his unconditioned figure. His t-shirts used to stretch a little across his body due to his broad chest. But now they did so due to a burgeoning pot belly. Devlin often used to run in the mornings when he was with Emma. He would push himself. Lactic acid would be replaced by endorphins. He would gulp down tap water as if it were liquid ambrosia. On his return, should Emma still be home as opposed to working in the florist, they would make love in the shower. The couple might then go to the park and just sit and read, with Violet curled up in between them. Contented.

Devlin left the house. He walked with his head down, as though he were a clergyman, deep in prayer. He had no desire to meet anyone's gaze. Connect. Should Devlin have looked up – and around – he might have spotted two CIA watchers following him. They hovered about at a distance, like a brace of vultures riding the thermals.

To further shutout the bleating world he inserted his headphones and turned the music up. At first, he switched on *Holly's Playlist*, a collection of songs his late wife used to listen to:

"Love has truly been good to me
Not even one sad day
Or minute have I had since you've come my way
I hope you know I'd gladly go
Anywhere you'd take me
It's so amazing to be loved
I'd follow you to the moon in the sky above."

The music conjured up all manner of memories for the widower. Lazy summer afternoons spent in Hyde park, resting her head on his chest like a pillow as they drank ice-cold lemonade and read pot-boiler novels. Illicit sex in women's changing rooms as she invited him in to see how an outfit looked on her. Sighing quietly yet intimately. She often told him how much she loved him, during or just after climaxing. Tears sometimes in her eyes. Sometimes giggly. Sometimes tingling or shaking. Sometimes desperately wanting to be hugged. On flights home from trips away she would lift the arm rest between them, lean into him and share the music she was listening to by dividing up her headphones. Holly was the only one he could ever talk to about how lonely his childhood was – and what it felt like to be abandoned by his natural parents. She would always remind him of how much he was loved now though, by his foster parents and herself.

Devlin's bittersweet reveries grew more painful however, as the wrack continued to turn. He changed the playlist. He pictured Holly again, lying in the hospital bed. Her comely features were swollen - bloody and ashen in different places, like the patina on a slab of marble. He closed his eyes and felt again the slight squeeze of her fingertips as he spoke to her, whist her life ebbed away – swirling down the drain. The doctor said it was a reflex action, but he believed otherwise. She was responding to his voice. There was still hope then. Faith. But that was then. The garrotte of grief continued to choke. But Devlin embraced the pain. It was all he had, or all that seemed real. True. It proved how much he loved her. That love exists in the world. This wicked, vain and plague-ridden world.

"If I could only turn back the clock to when God and her were born

Come in she said I'll give you shelter from the storm."

Devlin stood in Garratt Lane cemetery, staring at Holly's gravestone. An asphalt sky augured rain.

Vincent Cutter sat on a bench, in the distance, watching Devlin. The CIA operative, who had worked under Talbot for over five years, opened-up his laptop and updated his report on the Englishman. His orders were to just observe, unless it looked like Devlin was going to leave the country.

"Just get to know him. Make sure he isn't on drugs, or physically and mentally burned out. If he has any other weaknesses though, we can use them to strengthen our hand," Talbot instructed his agent.

Cutter was squarely built, but agile. Like a Humvee. His crew cut was severe, as often was his expression. The forty-year-old former marine was professional and precise in his conduct. The ardent patriot was loyal to his country and employer. His wife had come second to his job, which is why she divorced him. Talbot had taken Cutter under his wing, after the agent had failed the psych tests during his application to join the Secret Service. Talbot was his mentor – and even after five years Cutter would avidly listen to the older man's words of wisdom (he was also grateful for the regular bonus payments his handler gave him, outside his government salary):

"The rules of engagement should be shoot first, so that you only have to shoot once... Who needs to win hearts and minds when you have them by the balls?... Know your enemy, before he even knows you're his enemy... It's when you don't lie to Congress that they think something is wrong... Plausible deniability. They should always be your ultimate watchwords."

Cutter updated Talbot by leaving his report in a draft folder of an email account he shared with his employer - that way no correspondence was actually sent (and potentially intercepted). The CIA operative, or one of his colleagues, had been following their person of interest for a few days now. Cutter reported that the Englishman drank heavily. He spent several afternoons or evenings at his local pub. In terms of his routine he regularly walked his dog, visited his life wife's grave and attended to his ailing foster parent at a nursing home. He didn't work but rather lived off a generous income from monies earned as a contract killer. Having read about his service record in Afghanistan and some of the hits attributed to Devlin the agent granted the Englishman some grudging respect. He was a fellow professional. Talbot also read with interest about the events of the previous night. Any reservations the agent might have had about the target losing his edge had been quelled. The English hitman had ice in his veins, to face down the Jamaican gunman as he did. Or Devlin possessed a death wish. He certainly possessed good taste in women, the American thought, as he clicked open the photographs of Emma and Holly. Cutter briefly thought of an ex-girlfriend who had been crippled in a car accident recently, as he read about the death of Devlin's wife. *God only knows what the bastard went through.* Any admiration Cutter harboured for Devlin would not colour his judgement however should Talbot order him to take the Englishman out. He had killed better men, during sanctioned and unsanctioned operations. Talbot told him where to point – and Cutter fired. No questions asked.

Semper fidelis.

Devlin picked up a few pieces of litter, lying next to Holly's grave, and replaced the old bouquet of flowers with a new one. He read the inscription on the gravestone once more, a quote from Coleridge:

"To be beloved is all I need
And whom I love I love indeed."

The words had carved themselves into his soul, as surely as they were carved into the expensive marble. He spoke to her.

As much as Devlin knew what his wife would say to him back, he still would have loved to hear her voice again. Just once even.

If he had drawn another gun last night, I still would have walked towards him. I felt like I was walking towards you. I'm not sure I even confronted them out of a desire to save other people. In the end, we're all dead.

Devlin's phone vibrated in his pocket. Usually he turned it off, whilst talking to his wife, but as he was expecting a call from the care home about his father's latest blood test he checked the screen. He duly ignored it and placed the device back into his pocket on viewing the missed call – and then text message – from Birch.

"It's been a year. Let's celebrate."

John Birch had served with Devlin in Helmand – and had been injured during Rameen's attack on the village. Birch had also been the one to alert Devlin of the Afghan's presence in the London last year. He reminded the contract killer of his promise that he would kill Rameen, if ever the opportunity arose. Devlin wasn't in the mood to celebrate the anniversary however. He winced, as if he were in physical torment, as he remembered Tyerman. It was the anniversary of his death too. The sins of the past can cling to you, like leeches. Bleed you dry.

After visiting Holly's grave Devlin smoked a couple of cigarettes outside the gates of the cemetery and then flagged down a black cab to take him to the *Huntsman & Hound* pub. He needed a drink.

Cutter and his watch team followed in a charcoal grey BMW.

The *Huntsman & Hound* pub was located just off the Old Kent Rd. Black, iron horseshoes and yellowing photographs of how the pub looked in the past adorned the walls. The polished brass fittings and rows of glasses, hanging from the bar, gleamed in the improving sunshine. A smell of beer, chicken goujons and furniture polish infused the air.

A couple of locals sat at the far end of the bar, whilst a few medical students worked their way through a second bottle of wine in the corner. Devlin gave the locals a friendly nod and then caught the eye of Terry Gilby, the pub's genial landlord. Devlin made a subtle swirling motion of his finger, signalling that he was happy to buy a round of drinks for everyone.

Shortly afterwards the door to the pub opened and an American ordered a drink. He sat himself at a table, read the newspaper and glanced at his phone and watch – as if he was waiting for someone.

Devlin downed half his pint in a few desperate and thirst-quenching gulps. Frequenting the pub had become one of his few pleasures in life. He often took Violet along with him. It felt more like home than home.

"How 'ave you been?" Terry asked, confident that, unlike some of his other customers, Devlin wouldn't launch into a Jerimiah. The landlord had almost become the postcode's sin eater, listening to his patrons' various problems: marital issues, the ineptitude of the local council, work troubles, Millwall's loss of form and the rising price of cigarettes.

"I'm fine," Devlin casually replied, as if he didn't have a care in the world, as he also waved his hand in acknowledgement of the locals at the end of the bar thanking him for the drink. "How have you been? Busy?"

"Busy enough. When it gets quiet I often wish that it'll liven up. But when it gets busy I long for it to be quiet again," Terry replied in good humour, clinking his pewter tankard against his friend's. "L'chaim."

"L'chaim," Devlin enjoined – and finished off the remainder of his pint.

"So, did you hear about the shooting last night in Bermondsey Square? A yardie gunned down a couple of Albanians. And then the yardie was beaten to within an inch of his life by a mysterious bystander – with an ashtray of all things, according to some reports. There are worse tragedies. At least it wasn't another poxy terrorist attack. There's a chance you might have even heard the shots from your flat."

"I saw something on the news this morning but I wasn't really concentrating. I also slept through the whatever happened. I heard enough gunfire in Helmand to last me a lifetime. Hopefully the government might now be encouraged to bring back smoking in pubs, given the security benefits of ashtrays."

"Amen to that. You must have seen a lot during your time over there. Did you ever have to shoot at anyone? I won't be offended if you tell me to mind my own business," Terry said, as he poured his friend another pint. He subtly shook his head when Devlin motioned to pay, indicating that the drink was on the house.

"I fear I might bore you to sleep should I start recounting some old war stories. Suffice to say I fired off a few shots in anger, whilst over in Afghanistan. One of the councillors over in Helmand once asked a sniper what he felt, when he fired off a shot and killed an enemy. "Well, depending on if I haven't had breakfast that morning, I feel hungry," he replied... After the Iranian Embassy siege in the early eighties the SAS were all asked to submit a report of their actions during the assault. A soldier was quizzed as to why he shot a single terrorist more than thirty times. His answer: "I ran out of bullets." I knew soldiers in Helmand who discharged their weapons by accident, or out of nervousness. Others did so out of anger or a sense of vengeance for fallen comrades... If you don't shoot the enemy, the enemy will shoot you... Soldiering is a job. And controlled aggression is part of the job description... Sometimes war can bring out the best in people, sometimes it can bring out the worst..."

Devlin thought how, more than perhaps any other regiment, the Paras brought out the best and worst in people. The motto of the regiment was *Ready for Anything*. The Paras went forward when others would take a step back, or retreat. They fought for one another like brothers. Fearless. Often decent. Often noble. Montgomery had called the Paras, "Men apart." But Devlin had witnessed the darker side of "men apart" – behaving like animals. Few squaddies gained their red beret without a bout or two of milling. Devlin had stepped into the ring himself. He had been both a lion – and punchbag – at the same time. His arms hung off him like two sacks of potatoes afterwards. His expression creased in disgust every time he recalled the "gunge" contests of his fellow squaddies. Shit was eaten, piss was drunk. 1 Para prided itself on being the best, or worst, "gungers". The other great contest between squaddies, to separate the men from the boys or Paras from the craphats, during his time in the regiment had been the Dance of the Flaming Arseholes. Soldiers would strip naked, roll-up a magazine and shove it into their arse. It was then set on fire. As the rest of the room chanted a song called "The Zulu Warrior" the Para would dance on the table and try to let the magazine burn down as far as possible, until he couldn't endure the pain anymore. Devlin tried to remain a man apart on such nights. He would retire early and catch up on some reading, or maintain his weapon and kit.

"Truth as Circe: Error has transformed animals into men: is truth perhaps capable of turning man back into an animal?"

Devlin recalled the quote from Nietzsche as he remembered the incidents of beastings and punishments beatings throughout his training. Man's inhumanity to man is the dye that's impossible to whitewash from history. We're human, all too human after all. Devlin himself had executed Taliban fighters and turned a blind eye to acts of sadism. He still couldn't be sure if he lost or found himself during his tours. Most of the horror stories about what the Paras did to captured IRA members in the seventies also contained kernels of truth. But the IRA were also men apart, Devlin judged. Vile, brutal, conceited thugs – adopting a romantic cause to mask a criminal organisation which pedalled drugs and ran one of the largest protection rackets in Europe. When Devlin was offered the contract to take out a former IRA brigade commander he willingly accepted.

"Where's Kylie? Is she not working today?" Devlin asked, curious. He also wanted to steer the conversation away from his time in the army. It was another part of his past he wanted to bury. Kylie was a barmaid. Devlin had known her from when she used to work in *The Admiral Nelson*, a pub close to his flat. He had slept with her then. He had slept with her again, about a month ago. She had recently broken things off with her boyfriend. It had been late. They were both drunk. Both lonely. Devlin visited Holly's grave the following morning and said that it had meant nothing. A few days later Kylie was back with her fiancé. When Devlin and the barmaid saw each other again they duly acted as if nothing had happened.

"She asked for the day off. Her idiot and selfish shit of brother has taken what spare cash she has and disappeared again. She came in earlier, crying her eyes out, saying that Paul Simms and Chris Chard were demanding that she pay her brother's debts. If you didn't already know Simms and Chard work for Tony Jackson, the local loan shark and drug dealer. The two businesses complement each other. I'm not even sure if Tony knows that they're hassling Kylie for the money. It's not his style to go after women. Simms and Chard may be doing it to earn some extra cash, or they're just getting their kicks from terrorising her. I'd offer to help her out but her brother owes over five grand. She doesn't want to ask her fiancé either, in case it causes an argument and he break things off again."

Devlin compressed his jaw and pursed his lips. His stomach tightened into a fist. He pictured Kylie's heart-shaped face and bright, coquettish eyes. There wasn't a mean bone in her body. She couldn't afford five grand. But it didn't matter. Devlin would make somebody else pay.

"I think I've seen Simms and Chard about before. Do they still drink in *The Plough*, off Deptford High St?"

"Aye. Simms is shagging the landlady there. Hopefully she'll give him a dose of the clap and he'll be too ill hassle Kylie. Fancy another drink?"

"No, I best be off. I need to feed Violet and take her for a walk."

"Will you be back later?"

"I'm not sure. I need to take care of some business first."

5.

Devlin paced – or stalked - around his living room and smoked another cigarette. Music played in the background. After returning home Devlin had fed and walked his dog. He also cooked himself a meal of some grilled trout and steamed broccoli. He resisted the temptation of drinking a bottle of wine with dinner and just had water. He wanted to rehydrate and sober up. Be sharp.

Devlin remembered the brief look of rejection on Kylie's face when, as they lay in bed, she asked if things would ever get serious between them - and he replied that they couldn't. He then thought of Holly and turned his back to the barmaid. But the girl's hurt expression now scorched what was left of his soul. He hoped he would now be able atone for the hurt he caused. Absolve himself. Kylie would never know how he helped her. But that didn't matter. Devlin would know. God would too.

The ex-soldier told himself he wasn't suffering from bloodlust, having gained a taste of violence again from the previous night. It was just an unfortunate coincidence. *I'm still retired.* He didn't want to scratch the itch but he was left with no choice. Simms and Chard needed to pay.

And Devlin would be able to forgive himself for what he was about to do. Holly would forgive him too. If God was unable to forgive him, so be it. Devlin had still not been able to forgive Him for taking his wife away.

Devlin finished off his cigarette, retrieved the claw hammer from his tool box and headed out.

Years of soldiering had taught Devlin how to be patient. After having walked past the pub and confirmed that Simms and Chard were present he crossed the road and sat by the window in a late night Turkish kebab house. He ordered a coffee, mixed grill and read the newspaper, whilst keeping one eye on the doorway to *The Plough*.

A few cheers and jeers filled the restaurant as a group of young men sat and watched a Galatasaray match in the corner. But Devlin tuned them out. His eyes were as keen as a croupier's, keeping track of all the bets, as he focused on the job at hand and played out various scenarios. What if there was a lock-in at the pub and the two men stayed there for the night? What if they didn't leave together and went their separate ways immediately after leaving? What if they turned left together? What if they turned right? What was their likely route and destination?

The waitress, Helena, approached him again to re-fill his coffee. They had spoken earlier. She was a mature student, studying European Literature, and worked in the restaurant at night to help pay her tuition fees. "I'm giving myself a second chance in life, trying to better myself," Helena remarked. They briefly chatted about Balzac and Flaubert. She was impressed. He was courteous, attractive and, from the looks of his watch, wealthy. Helena was a blend of Asiatic and Arabic good looks. Long, glossy black hair hung down her back like silk drapes. She was alluring, even in dark jeans and a cheap t-shirt (with the name of the kebab house, *Kebabylon*, emblazoned across it).

"Anything interesting in the newspaper?"

"It's all bad news I'm afraid, aside from the fact that one of the stars from a programme called Made in Chelsea has died of a drug overdose," Devlin drily joked. He figured that anyone who liked Balzac would have a healthily dark sense of humour. "It's the only bit of news they're not blaming on Brexit. Although I'm sure someone will write into the letters page and correct that mistake."

Helena laughed and her lips curled-up into a cat-like smile.

"You have nice, kind eyes," she suddenly and flirtatiously expressed, surprising herself a little by how forward she was. Usually the customers hit on her. But here she was chatting a customer up.

"I'm sure it's just a trick of the light," Devlin replied.

"You're modest too."

"I have a lot to be modest about, unfortunately"

Helena laughed again - and tucked her hair behind her ear.

"I'll be taking my break soon. Would it be okay to sit with you for a while?"

Devlin was tempted. Perhaps it was time he started dating again. Enjoying himself. He was attracted to her. It had been a year since he had shared a nourishing conversation over a nice meal. He would enjoy making love to her, going on holiday together. Visiting art museums and seeing plays. Spending the night on the sofa, watching a film. Laughing.

But Devlin had a job to do tonight. As well as Helena, standing in front of him, an image of Kylie came into his mind. Duty called.

"I'm afraid that I might have to suddenly leave soon, I'm due to meet someone," Devlin politely replied, placing his hand on the table so that his wedding ring came into view.

The waitress said she understood – and forced a smile – before retreating to the counter.

Devlin left Helena a tip which was equal to the price of his meal and drinks – and headed out into the street, having spotted Simms and Chard leaving *The Plough*. He decided to keep his distance to begin with. As he crossed the street he noticed a brace of rats scuttling along the curb and was reminded of something one of the regulars, a pest control officer, said in the *Huntsman & Hound* a week ago:

"You can't kill every rat. You need to accept them, like the air you breathe. To even get close to wiping them all out you'd have to use so much poison that you'd probably kill off half the good burghers of London too."

The street lighting was poor as they walked towards the *Pankhurst* housing estate but Devlin was still able to take in his prey. Simms possessed a pasty complexion, even in summer. He was gaunt, rake thin and swaggered rather than walked, imitating the gait of some of his favourite rap artists. Although approaching forty Simms was still dressed in a tracksuit, baseball cap and a pair of garish Puma trainers. Simms had been dealing – and consuming – drugs since his mid-teens. He was far from the best advert for taking weed and coke – given his unpleasant character and appearance – but Simms knew his business and customer base. Most of the sentences that came out of Simms' mouth contained two – or three – swear words. The small man liked to play the big man. He was relentless and ruthless when it came to collecting debts for his boss, Tony Jackson. The first warning was merely verbal. But should a customer not pay the required sum on the second time of asking Simms would pull out his knife and slice the webbing on his victim's fingers. On the third time of asking Simms unleashed Chard. Thumbs or arms were broken. Goods were also removed from the debtor's home. Simms was also proficient at carrying out his boss' orders of occasionally giving his product away for free.

"Concentrate on getting them hooked first. Sooner or later we'll make them pay double. And if they can't quite afford to do so, we can happily lend them the money of course," the rapacious Jackson instructed, providing a business plan for his small army of dealers and enforcers.

The brawny Chard dwarfed his friend, almost comically so. He wore a Paul Shark jacket over a chequered Ben Sherman shirt, elasticated jeans to cater for his large waist and a Dunn & Co flat cap, which had once belonged to his costermonger father. Ten years of boxing gave the enforcer a flat, crooked nose and cauliflower ears. His neck was thick, his hands were as large as bear paws and his knuckles scarred. When the big man hit someone, he stayed hit. Either sinus trouble, or an addiction to cocaine, caused the enforcer to constantly sniff.

Devlin made an educated guess that the pair were ultimately cutting through the housing estate to reach a late-night bar on Deptford High St. He made the decision to break off following the two men – and took a different path through the estate – having settled on a narrow alleyway where he could ambush his prey. There would be no room for the two men to manoeuvre or escape. The passage was situated between the estate's generator and one of the walls of the children's playground. No one could look out their window and witness the attack, should they hear any screams.

He reached his destination, hiding just behind the generator at the mouth of the passageway, and waited. He knew he wouldn't have to wait long. Devlin, like a number of other soldiers or criminals he had encountered over the years, possessed an internal switch - a kill switch – which he could turn on at will to get the job down. Violence and immorality became a necessity. Doubt, decency, cowardice and conscience were all switched off. They would be fine to be switched on again, after the job was finished.

Devlin heard their voices and footsteps approaching. He took a breath and gripped the pimpled handle of the claw hammer. Holly had bought him the hammer, as part of a toolbox, many years ago. He had used it to hammer in the nails to hang-up various works of art.

He was wearing black jeans, a black shirt and dark blue summer blazer, with a spacious inside pocket. Devlin had retrieved the balaclava from his pocket and placed it over his head. The soles of his shoes were rubber, having had them changed from the original leather, lest he slipped and lost his footing. The devil is in the detail.

It was dark. The attacker owned the element of surprise. And the victims' reflexes were dulled from drink and drugs. Devlin paused not to let his opponents take him in as he appeared before them.

Chard was first hit with a powerful kick to the groin. He was winded, disorientated – in too much pain to retaliate. Before Simms had a chance to react Devlin grabbed the spindly drug dealer and smashed his head against a brick wall – just forcefully enough to knock him down rather than out.

As Chard began to straighten-up and absorb things he received another agonising blow to the groin. This time the big man fell. Devlin quickly snatched the flat cap from his head and placed it over his mouth as he pounded the hammer on his kneecaps. Once. Twice. His large body jolted, from head to toe, with each savage blow.

Devlin muffled the screams but then removed the cap and loomed over the stricken enforcer. Tears moistened his eyes.

He seethed and puffed out his cheeks. His knees – legs – felt like they were on fire.

"Keep quiet. If you make a sound or move I'll crush your windpipe. Nod if you understand."

Chard grimaced and nodded.

Devlin swiftly transferred his attention back to Simms. Blood seeped out of the back of his throbbing head and stained his baseball cap. He was just coming out of his daze when he felt his attacker remove his trainers. Devlin removed a sock too and forced Simms to insert it into his mouth, threatening to smash his teeth in if he failed to comply. The eyes looking out from the balaclava were far from kind.

There are over twenty-five bones in a human foot. Devlin broke most of them as he ferociously struck both of Simms' feet, like a blacksmith pounding on his anvil. Bone and cartilage snapped like bracken. The drug dealer's remaining cream sock quickly turned red. Simms moaned, twisted and turned – but to no avail.

"You tell Jackson that Deptford now belongs to Spinks," Devlin remarked, speaking loudly and forcefully through the balaclava. Spinks was a rival operator to Jackson, whose territory encompassed Woolwich and Thamesmead. Devlin calculated that Jackson might retaliate and start a war. Hopefully the two men would go to war. It was a dog eat dog world. But either way he was confident Kylie would be free from suspicion, as to the being the origin of the attack.

Devlin relieved the two men of their mobile phones and a large roll of cash. He walked away, wiping away any spots of blood from the hammer and his hands. The assault had taken no more than two minutes – but it's legacy would endure. Simms would now hobble, rather than swagger. Chard would also be out of action for some time. Jackson might even write his two employees off – and demand payment for the money Devlin took from them.

As he reached the high street and flagged down a cab his phone vibrated with a message, from Porter.

"We need to talk."

Devlin messaged back that he would call his friend in the morning. He renewed the promise he made to himself however:

I'm still retired.

It had been like old times. Before his retirement. Porter had returned from London and lied to his wife about his day. He had met with Talbot but said to Victoria that he had visited *Farlows* in Piccadilly and ordered new fishing rods and tackle (he had bought various pieces of equipment online to give credence to his story). Porter wasn't a proud liar, he was just a proficient one, he thought. He came through the door early evening and forced a smile, pretending that all was well. For her part Victoria pretended not to notice that there was something that her husband wasn't telling her. Just like old times.

Victoria rested on her bed. A book lay open in front of her but she couldn't concentrate. The words seemed dead on the page. She bit her nails and felt like clasping the cross around her neck. And praying. She imagined how her pragmatic husband would have argued that praying wouldn't do any good. But she would have countered that it couldn't do any harm either.

Porter sat at the dining room table downstairs. He wanted some time alone, to brood, think, frown and hold his head in his hands. The fixer only forced a smile when his dog, Marlborough, nuzzled his leg and whimpered – either in sympathy with his master or the hound heard the fox padding across the lawn outside.

His phone buzzed. Porter read the text message from Devlin, to say that he would call in the morning. He wished he could have kept his friend out of Talbot's plans – but he was central to them. Both men would meet with the American tomorrow. He was too tired, or despondent, to think of another deception tonight to tell Victoria, to explain away another trip to London.

Porter downed another mouthful of brandy and took another drag on his cigar. But he took little pleasure in his familiar vices. They delivered little consolation. He felt like his head was in a noose – and Talbot's hand was on the lever which worked the trapdoor. His could lose everything. For once the fixer was at another man's mercy. Porter was used to manipulating events, not being manipulated himself. Suffice to say he preferred the former. Only Devlin could save him. He needed to say yes to Talbot's proposal. Do the job. Porter knew that he had to help save Devlin in return however. He was his brother's keeper.

6.

Devlin called Porter first thing in the morning. On the surface of things the conversation was a normal one. Porter mentioned a time and location to meet – to discuss a possible business opportunity. At the beginning of the exchange however Porter asked about the health of his foster parent, which was a pre-arranged code between the two associates to signal that one of their phones or emails might be being monitored.

Devlin hung up, briefly closed his eyes and sighed.

We are where we are.

He walked and fed Violet, whilst idly speculating on his forthcoming meeting with Porter. No amount of money could tempt him to come out of retirement, he determined. He no longer owned a weapon. He could no longer be a gun for hire. Out of a courtesy to his friend he would meet with Porter though. He owed him that. The tone of his voice suggested that it might be something different to the fixer offering him a contract as well, especially since he still thought Porter was enjoying his retirement. It was not completely out of the ordinary for his former employer to enact the simple security protocol. But it was rare. Better to be safe than sorry, Porter would argue.

Midday. The address Porter gave Devlin was for a house on Boston Place, close to Baker St tube station. The property was large but anonymous looking. He rang the bell. His heart beat a little faster than normal but Devlin's expression remained impassive. He was briefly tempted, earlier in the morning, to bring a weapon to the meeting but he trusted his friend. There were other protocols Porter could have enacted in a coded way. He could have warned Devlin that he was in danger, or to get out the country immediately, through various pre-arranged phrases.

Cutter opened the heavy black door and invited Devlin in with a nod of his head.

"Raise your arms please," the American instructed, neither politely nor rudely, before padding the visitor down for any concealed firearms. "If you could also remove your phone and any other electronic devices from your pockets."

Devlin left his phone in the allotted plastic container on a table by the door. Cutter pulled out a paddle-shaped scanner and ran it over the Englishman's person, checking for cameras or bugs. As the agent did so Devlin caught a glimpse of the man's Glock 43 beneath his suit jacket. Or perhaps Cutter allowed him to catch a glimpse of the weapon, as a threat or warning. Devlin remained unfazed by the rigmarole and security procedures. He'd experienced them plenty of times before.

Cutter scrutinised Devlin, looking for signs of shock, surprise or fear. But the hitman remained unreadable - unhackable.

The agent led Devlin upstairs to a clean, spacious living room, where Porter and Talbot were waiting.

"Good afternoon Mr. Devlin. I hope I can call you Michael. My name is Mason Talbot. I work for the CIA, for my sins. Oliver will be able to vouch for my credentials and character. Thank you for meeting with me on such short notice. Firstly, would you like something to eat or drink? Vincent here can get you something," Talbot amiably remarked, smiling on more than once occasion. Hopefully everything could be civil. Or as civil as humanly possible - in light of the blackmail and other crimes which were about to take place.

"I'm fine, thanks."

Devlin glanced around the smartly furnished room. A big, flat screen tv next to a cabinet full of DVDs dominated one corner. A blood-red Dyson air purifier hummed in another corner. A row of bestselling paperbacks sat over an ornamental fireplace. Porter was sitting on one of two expensive, comfortable leather sofas which faced one another. The blinds had been pulled down over the windows and the room was illuminated by a pair of tall, brass floor lamps.

Inoffensive works of art hung on the walls. Family photographs and personal effects were absent. Devlin figured that the property was usually used as a safehouse.

As well as quickly surveying the room Devlin took in his host. White. Anglo-Saxon. Protestant. The American was well-groomed and well-conditioned. He was dressed in a navy-blue Brooks Brothers suit, pristine white shirt and red silk tie (held in place with a gold, but not garish, tie pin). His shoes were as polished as the wooden floor he was standing on. Devlin caught a whiff of both cologne and moisturiser on the senior CIA agent. He looked good, even great, for his age. His voice was clear and authoritative. He could have been an American news anchor for Fox News (as opposed to CNN). Devlin suspected that his forehead had been botoxed on more than one occasion – and that the agent bleached his teeth. Talbot was not so much a car salesman, as someone who owned an entire dealership, Devlin later considered.

Porter stood-up and greeted his friend. He appeared a little sheepish. Outfoxed. His expression was creased in worry – or contrition – as he shook Devlin's hand. Porter somehow seemed diminished, deferent, in the American's presence.

"It's good to see you again, Michael," Porter said. It remained obvious, but unsaid, that he wished it was under different circumstances.

Devlin nodded, in a non-committal way, in reply.

"Please, gentlemen, take a seat. My apologies, Oliver, if I repeat some of what we discussed during our previous meeting. You seem like a straight talking – as well as straight shooting – kind of man, Mr. Devlin. As such I will come straight to the point. I want you to carry out a job for me."

"I'm retired," Devlin remarked, not quite rudely but matter-of-factly.

Talbot smiled in reply, almost unctuously, as though he had won a private bet with himself as to predicting the Englishman's reaction to his opening salvo.

"I think you might find that you've just been on a long sabbatical. It was Oliver's first thought too. But then, wisely, he had second thoughts when I made him an offer he couldn't refuse, to quote a phrase."

Devlin turned to look at Porter, who was sitting beside him on the sofa, but the fixer averted his gaze and bowed his head, in shame or otherwise.

"You only have yourself to blame, one might argue," Talbot continued, after taking a sip of coffee and fastidiously smoothing his tie down. "You came to my attention as a result of your last job. Your principle target was Rameen Jamal, I believe. But you also took out Faisal Ahmadi, a person of interest to me. Incidentally, I was surprised, impressed or appalled by you shooting your former commanding officer that night. In another lifetime I would have gazumped Oliver and recruited you myself, when you left the army. But as to Ahmadi it was my intention to turn him, or at least extract sufficient intelligence from the agent. I wanted to know who his paymasters were – and who he was giving money to. You rendered my operation obsolete however. Ahmadi's death didn't upset me, God and Allah knows the cretin deserved to die. But I found it irksome, to say the least, when some cowboy moseyed on into *The Ritz* and gunned down my target. I do not like to have my time and energies wasted. Now you and Oliver here were clever enough to shut down the surveillance systems of the hotel during the hit. But our equipment was still working fine when you entered and exited the building. Man plans, God laughs. It took some time but we managed to track you down. We duly discovered your connection to Oliver and I built up a file on you both. I've condensed the highlights of your files into these two folders, which you can peruse before you leave. Or you may want to glance at them now, so you are fully aware of the unfortunate position you're in."

With a nod of his head Talbot instructed Cutter to hand over the two manila folders, containing photographs, intelligence reports and facsimiles of bank records and other documents. The CIA operative had been thorough. He often compared his agency to "the great Eye of Sauron," which saw and knew everything, eventually.

"I have considered you both prospective assets for some time. You just didn't know it. I felt fine to put you on ice, until now. I want you to help me make a problem disappear. Once done, those files you are holding will similarly disappear. Now before you think of chirping up and saying that you are still retired, Michael, I want you to think carefully not just about yourself, but think of others in your life too. The authorities can use what's in that binder to freeze and appropriate all your assets. A long prison sentence is inevitable. Who will then pay for your father's care home? Who will visit him in your place – and give him his cigarettes and navy rum? Your former girlfriend, Emma, will be devastated too. Not just because of a sense of betrayal and humiliation. But did you know she is currently applying to work for an NGO, dealing with foreign aid? How much would you rate her chances of success once the word gets out that she was intimately involved with a contract killer? And who will be left to tend to Holly's grave, after you're gone? Should you insist that you are still retired there will be consequences for Oliver, your partner in crime so to speak, as well. I'm not sure how much he – or his family - will enjoy his sunshine years from a drear jail cell. I take no pleasure in mentioning such unpleasantness but I believe it's best that you are apprised of all the facts before you make your final decision," Talbot remarked with sympathy. Unrepentantly.

Devlin remained outwardly calm – but inside he experienced an urge to make the CIA agent his next target. But that would only make his situation worse. He flicked through the pages of the file to discover photos of him leaving both Bermondsey Square and the *Pankhurst* estate. Perhaps if he still insisted that he was retired the American would threaten to send the relevant photos to the local yardie boss – and Jackson. His family – and the likes of Emma, Terry and Kylie – could suffer a worse fate than just seeing him go to prison. *And what would happen to Violet?*

Devlin always knew the past would somehow catch up with him one day. Perhaps the past caught up with him every day. It wasn't even the past. It was his present. We are where we are.

The past can, like malaria, lay dormant for years. But every decade or so the disease will rear its ugly head. Make you suffer.

7.

Devlin agreed to take on the job.

Talbot rubbed his hands in satisfaction and beamed, as if he had just closed a business deal of mutual benefit to all parties.

"I'm pleased, gentlemen, that we are all on the same page. You'll also be pleased that your target is neither a good nor innocent man, although we have all worked in this trade too long to grow a conscience. You are familiar with Ewan Slater..."

Porter pictured the fifty-year-old former MP for Bradford West. He was scruffy-chic and could often be seen wearing a corduroy cap, which he claimed had once belonged to John Lennon (although he had been quoted years ago as saying the cap belonged to Donovan). A former trade unionist and member of the Labour Party, Slater had run as an independent candidate a decade ago and, against all odds, had won a seat. He called his party "Vision." He had only served one term as an MP but Slater was currently experiencing a renaissance in support, mainly due to his appearance on the television show Strictly Come Dancing. He was willing to make a fool of himself – and a large section of the audience loved him for it. Vision was gaining some traction in the polls again and Slater had just announced that he would put himself forward as a candidate in the next election (albeit he remained coy about which constituency he would be running in). The BBC seemed to grant him as much favourable coverage as he desired and his team were adept at using social media (both to spread positive stories and shout down any critics). Most critics of the party were trolled and labelled "fascists" or "racists". *The Observer* half-jokingly described Ewan Slater as "slightly to the left of Jeremy Corbyn". The article also stated how the "socialist Nigel Farage" had won a poll relating to which political figure the public would most wish to have a drink with down the pub (despite the fact that Slater was a teetotaller). Porter had once met the rabble-rouser at a dinner in Mansion House. He was the guest of the Venezuelan ambassador. Porter had noticed over the years that even the most ardent communists were happy to break bread with capitalists, providing the spread was lavish enough and they didn't have to pay. Slater turned to championing his friend's country and its political system, arguing that "Venezuela is the fairest nation on Earth. Nigh on everyone is the same." Porter was tempted to reply, "Aye, nigh on everyone is poor and is an enemy of the state," - but desisted.

Talbot continued with his character assassination:

"Slater is vegetarian, against foxhunting and has spoken of a worldwide Jewish conspiracy on more than one occasion. He also fanatically believes the state should control the means of production. And he has the audacity to compare Donald Trump to Hitler. I am not at liberty to divulge the reason why we have commissioned this job but suffice to say you will be doing your country a great service. Slater may well be the single most dangerous man in Britain right now."

Porter painted a scenario of the target's resurgent party winning a few seats at the next election (in northern towns and constituencies encompassing large student populations). He would be able to prop-up a Labour government, if the polls were correct, in exchange for enacting certain policies and being given a prominent post in the cabinet. Slater's avowed enemy was "western imperialism". Capitalism was to blame for all the worlds' sins, according to the activist's political philosophy (although what Slater really desired to propagate was a political religion). He called *Das Kapital* his Bible and Marx was a prophet. The proletariat were the chosen people and socialism, national or otherwise, was the promised land. In terms of who should play the role of God, the evangelical atheist had no doubt pencilled himself in for the role. But only he had the vision to make things work. He could be a new Mao or Stalin, but he would learn from their mistakes. The CIA couldn't countenance such a figure having influence over foreign or trade policy relating to the United States, Porter mused. For years the establishment had rightly treated the radical socialist as a joke. Ewan Slater couldn't be afforded to have the last laugh however.

The CIA couldn't be caught carrying out an assassination of such a figure on British soil, Porter reasoned. Devlin provided them with plausible deniability. He was their scapegoat. A patsy.

"You have both been in the game long enough to know that, if apprehended, you will be on your own. And should you feel tempted to divulge any inappropriate information your families will suffer a far worse fate than just some financial insecurity."

Talbot hardened his features briefly – and Devlin fancied that he looked a little like a gargoyle - but then donned his mask of civility again. For the most part, the Englishmen sat in silence, like two chastised but truculent schoolboys outside the Headmaster's office. They would be unhappy about it – but they would take their punishment. Cutter brought a bottle and glass of wine over.

"This is your favourite Burgundy is it not, Oliver?" Talbot remarked, as an aside. His intention however was to stress to Porter just how much he knew about his new associate – and therefore control him.

Despite ashtrays being conspicuous by their absence – and Talbot pulling a face when the Englishman retrieved his cigarettes – Devlin lit-up and filled the pine and cranberry scented room with smoke. For his own sense of worth, he needed to assert his will and defy the arrogant CIA agent. Even it if was a meaningless victory.

"Now I appreciate how you have planned your jobs in the past but this operation has a strict time frame. Our window of opportunity will be open in two days. But rest assured the plan is sound. Should you have any reservations – or you discern any holes in the operation – we will duly listen. But Cutter will serve Slater up on a plate for you. We will provide you with a clean weapon. You will just need to arrange for your own extraction. But that shouldn't be a problem for you to fix, Oliver. Who knows, this could be the first of many jobs together. We could form our own special relationship... Cutter will brief you further on the details. We have a file on Slater, which we can show you. I want you to have full disclosure. In terms of intelligence, what's mine is yours. But I am afraid I need to leave, to attend another important meeting. No rest for the wicked. If a shark stops swimming, it dies," Mason Talbot confidentially exclaimed, like a man in control of his own fate - and the fate of others.

Cutter was thorough and professional in his briefing. The former Guards officer and ex-Para rolled back the years – and were under orders again like common soldiers. Cutter provided them with maps and laid out when and where Devlin would execute the kill shot. He had done most of Devlin's work for him, including recommending an escape route.

"I have studied your service record and other hits that we've attributed to you. You are more than capable of making the required shot."

The American ran through a list of rifles, suppressors and sights he could furnish the Englishman with, depending on his preference. All would be untraceable, should Devlin need to abandon the equipment during his exfiltration. Devlin also requested he be provided with a handgun – a Sig Sauer P226 – for the operation. Cutter paused to consider the request but then assented to it.

"We will meet again here for a final run through, the day after tomorrow. If you have any questions, now is the time to ask. Mr. Talbot and I do not tolerate failure or disloyalty. But you are both smart and professional enough to already know that, I imagine," the operative asserted, martinet-like, with more than a hint of warning in his voice. His expression was as taut as a bowstring.

"Rest assured, Mr. Cutter, I have no intention of ruining what Mr Talbot called our special relationship."

Yet.

8.

"Drink?" Porter suggested, mustering what little cheer he could in his being, as the two men stood outside the house on Boston Place.

"I wouldn't say no," Devlin replied, with understatement.

They headed down into the tube in order to employ some counter surveillance measures and shake off any watchers. It didn't really much matter whether they had a tail or not now but it was another small act of defiance. Travelling by tube again reminded Porter why he couldn't abide travelling by tube. He turned his nose up at the odours, as well as the ill-mannered and ill-dressed passengers. *The great unwashed*, he snobbishly thought, quoting Cicero to himself.

The pair alighted at Oxford St where Porter bought a couple of mobile phones. They decided that the best way to communicate over the next few days would be via *Whatsapp*. The system was nigh on impossible to crack, even for the intelligence services. After leaving the phone shop Porter hailed a black cab and instructed the driver to take them to the Special Forces Club in Knightsbridge.

Porter was a member of several clubs in London – including The Garrick, The Athenaeum, White's and The Savile Club. Although he seldom now used the Special Forces Club he was warmly greeted by one of the managers as he entered the establishment. The spic and span figure resembled Capt. Peacock from *Are You Being Served?* Devlin fancied.

"Afternoon Mr. Porter. It is good to see you again. I hope you're keeping well. Thank you so much for the signed and personalised copy of the Frank Kitson book. It's much appreciated."

There were some things which Oliver Porter still didn't mind fixing.

The two men went upstairs, ordered a couple of drinks and sat in the corner.

"I'm sorry, Oliver," Devlin exclaimed, his expression contrite and pained. If not for Devlin's insistence on carrying out the hit on Rameen Jamal then they wouldn't be in their current parlous state.

Porter waved his hand in front of his face, as if brushing away a fly. Part of him was indeed upset with his friend but the blame game wouldn't do anyone any good at present. Pragmatism was the order of the day.

"What's done is done. We need to concentrate on the job at hand and make sure we can extricate ourselves from acting as assets for our American cousins in the future. I have no desire to sell my soul to Mason Talbot. As little as my soul may be worth, I warrant it's worth more than that. His leverage will remain, once we've completed the hit. A small mercy may be that he's intending to return to the US next year, to run for Congress. But that doesn't mean he won't turn over our files to his replacement."

Devlin nodded his head in acknowledgment, agreement. But his face betrayed a sense of resignation to his drear fate. All is for the worst in the worst in the worst of all possible worlds, he morbidly thought.

"We're going to have to complete this job," Porter continued, as he fastidiously straightened the cutlery on the table in front of him. "Are you confident of making the shot?"

"That won't be a problem. It seems strange that they would want to kill Slater in such dramatic fashion though. They could easily engineer things, given an extended time frame, to make it look like an accident."

"There does seem to be something else going on. Surely Talbot cannot consider Slater to be such a dangerous figure, who could have such an adverse effect on America's interest? The election is some time away. It's more fantasy than reality at the moment that Slater would be in a position to do a deal with Labour and get into power," Porter posited, thinking how he would look into any personal connection Talbot had with their target. Something was amiss.

"And will you be fine to arrange our extraction?"

"Mariner should be able to immobilise any local CCTV, if needed. I'll also contact Danny Tanner to organise a vehicle. He should be able to dispose of the car and weapons at a designated drop-off point too. I'm actually relieved that we'll be responsible for arranging our exit. I don't wholly trust our new friends. But tell me, how have you been keeping?" Porter asked, emitting a different type of concern in his voice.

"I've been better and I've been worse," Devlin answered, shrugging his shoulders slightly. He'd certainly been better, though he was at pains to remember a time when things had been worse. "And how's the family?"

For the first time that day a fond smile shaped Porter's features as the image of his wife and children came to mind.

"They're well, thank you. They're doing far better than I am at present it seems. Have you heard from Emma?" he asked, in hope more than expectation.

"Emma's due to visit the flat tomorrow, strangely enough, to pick up some papers which she left there. I'm planning to be out when she comes around though. She's engaged to be married. And you just heard today how she's applying for a new job. I'm happy for her. She's moved on," Devlin remarked, but a twinge of anguish sliced through his expression as he pictured his ex-girlfriend's face.

"And have you moved on? Do you have anyone special in your life?"

Devlin was tempted to reply that he had Holly, but he merely shook his head.

Porter took in his friend once more. He was like a worn piece of carpet, where the pattern could no longer be discerned.

"Are you keeping busy? Are you working on anything at the moment?"

Devlin nearly replied that he was working his way through half a bottle of Talisker a day.

"Fitzgerald said that there are no second acts in American lives," Porter continued. "But he didn't say anything about British lives. You'll find someone else, Michael."

"I know," Devlin solemnly replied, lying.

9.

The two men had a quick lunch and took their leave. Porter needed to get home and fix various things. For the first time in a long time he would work in his office in the garden.

Devlin took a cab home but then decided to get out prematurely at the Elephant & Castle. He needed some air. He resisted the temptation of stopping off at the *Charlie Chaplin* pub for a few drinks. As many sorrows as he had to drown he needed a clear head. He walked the rest of the way home, collecting his thoughts. He felt like he was in a maze – and he hadn't even reached the centre yet, let alone found a way out. Before, when plying his trade as a soldier or contract killer, he had the semblance of a choice to pull the trigger. But this was worse than his time in the army, when he had killed for a cause (however misguided that cause may have been). He had also killed to prevent the enemy from shooting himself and his friends. And as a hitman he had selected his targets. But now he was being forced to take another man's life. He was trapped, like a performing monkey in a cage. He wasn't scared of prison, or even solitary confinement, but he couldn't countenance making Bob or Emma pay for his sins.

Devlin told himself that he had killed better men than Slater, as well as worse, and that the self-serving politician deserved to die.

When he got back to his apartment Devlin checked beneath his carpet, to see if the crisps he had left there had broken beneath a trespasser's foot. Similarly, he checked if the ash he had left on part of his laptop had been disturbed. He swept for bugs and cameras on a device Porter had given him a couple of years ago. The flat was clean. But Talbot had little need to surveil Devlin now anyway. He had him where he wanted him.

After walking Violet along the river Devlin grabbed a bottle of water from the fridge and researched Ewan Slater on his computer.

The politician had been born in Mells, an affluent village in Somerset. His father had been a senior civil servant, his mother a ceramics teacher. Despite his self-proclaimed solidarity with "the ordinary, working man" Slater was schooled at Harrow and Keble College, Oxford. After university, he joined various activist and militant organisations, including the League Against Cruel Sports and the Surrey Socialist Chapter. His general political stance throughout the years, which remained either nobly or stubbornly consistent, was that the state should aim to curb, or abolish, capitalism. The establishment directed world affairs – started wars, caused economic crashes, rigged elections through the media – to keep themselves in power (Slater also hinted on occasion that the world was directed by a cabal of Jews, as opposed to American capitalists). Government should control the means of production. The state should also punitively – or "fairly" – tax anyone in a higher income bracket to himself. The people with the broadest shoulders should bear the heaviest burden. "It should be a crippling burden," Slater had even once venomously remarked off air, whilst his microphone was still on. The former editor of the *Morning Star* implemented a U-turn recently however on his proposed policy to target highly paid footballers – blaming them for all that was wrong with society. He dropped his proposals of a special wealth tax after his Director of Communications ran several focus groups on the issue, which concluded that the policy wasn't gaining traction. He duly reverted to blaming bankers and "fat cats" for the country's woes. "The most important challenge facing this country is battling against the few, who oppress the many. Trade Unionists – and the activists involved in organisations like Vision – must man the barricades and fight the good fight."

Slater's first wife was Katerina Schiller, who, it was rumoured, had strong ties to the Baader Meinhof gang in the nineteen seventies. Together they had one son, Rupert, who attended one of the country's top grammar schools (despite it being party policy that grammar schools should be abolished). Also, despite the charges of cronyism and nepotism that Slater levelled at the establishment, Rupert worked as an assistant to the leader's number two in Vision, Pat Snyde – the fair-weather Marxist and apologist for Sinn Fein.

Katerina divorced Slater in the mid-eighties. She claimed that the prominent member of CND and Amnesty International physically abused her during their marriage. Slater even, allegedly, punched his wife and broke her jaw on the night of Thatcher's landslide victory in 1987. Although the final settlement was undisclosed, it was said that Slater had to withdraw money from his family's trust fund to finance the alimony – and he was kept from selling the family pile, Cypress Manor, by the skin of his teeth.

Slater's second wife, who he was still married to, was the journalist Stella Brighton. When Owen Jones wasn't available, Sky News would call her up for her passionate and progressive viewpoints. For years Brighton had worked as an ardent campaigner for LGBT rights, gender equal pay and the criminalisation of all forms of hunting (including fishing). All the great and important issues of our time. She had an enviable amount of twitter followers and would often boast, whilst at the same time play the victim, about how she had received death threats online from trolls. But she would not be silenced, unfortunately. Brighton's focus of campaigning in the last year had revolved around visiting Syrian migrant camps (but only if she could be filmed at them and the BBC paid her expenses and a modest fee). On more than one occasion Brighton had stated how she would be willing to take in a migrant refugee family. "It's the humane thing to do." When a journalist recently asked her why she had still failed to take in anyone, or even apply to do so, the self-titled "neo-feminist" tetchily countered that, "this tragedy isn't just about me – you should focus on the big picture... There are children dying... You should be ashamed of yourself... As my husband recently said, the refugee crisis is the most important single issue facing the country today."

The refugee crisis was last years' news though. Her next crusade would be against (white) people guilty of cultural appropriation. She was already in talks with Channel 4 about a documentary. She had been tempted to address the subject of female genital mutilation, but her husband would need the Muslim vote in the forthcoming general election.

The couple made a formidable team, in terms of gaining air time. Brighton's Irish brogue and time spent being bi-sexual ticked plenty of diversity boxes. It helped that several of their friends from university now worked at *The Guardian* and the BBC as well. Ewan Slater's star was shining bright, since Strictly Come Dancing. The politician made the front page of the Sunday papers for the first time in his career, dressed up in a fat suit as the Prince, from Beauty and the Beast. After being voted off the programme he had brought in an image consultant to sharpen up his act - and softened some of his more radical views. During a recent interview with *The Independent* a reporter had done his homework and challenged Slater about some of his previous opinions and affiliations. During the eighties the activist had taken part in fund raising rallies for the IRA – and stated that any soldier who had participated in the Falkland's conflict should be prosecuted for war crimes. Israel was also "a stain upon the world's conscience" – and that "Stalin is the most misunderstood figure of the 20th century." Slater's reply was to argue that the reporter should, "Look to the future rather than dwell upon what was allegedly said the past. Most of this is fake news... A vote for Vision is a vote for hope. I want to see a new kind of politics. That's the most important thing you should convey to your readers. I want to be judged by the electorate - the kind of people who watch Strictly Come Dancing - not the right-wing media."

When the subject of Slater's party came up the journalist raised a couple of issues. Firstly, had he been aware that the BBC were sitting on a documentary exposing how Vision had targeted certain anti-Israel student bodies to recruit and campaign for the party? Also, was he aware of the fact that members of Vision were briefing students on how to vote twice in the general election, both in the constituency of their university and that of where their family home was located? Slater denied any knowledge of the documentary and remarked, for the record, that voter fraud was a crime: "Young people are our future. We should invest in them, not criticise them." In reply to allegations of anti-Semitism among party members Slater was forthright in his condemnation of any form of prejudice: "Vision has a zero-tolerance policy on such misdemeanours and will expel any party member guilty of hate speech or anti-Semitism." When asked how many members had been expelled in the past Slater replied that he didn't have the figures to hand. The answer was later found out to be none.

Devlin's search of images for Ewan Slater brought up an array of photographs of him shaking hands with "edgy" (but politically correct) stand-up comedians and past performers from the Cambridge Footlights. When he stubbed out another cigarette Devlin wished he could stub out half the world. Or himself. He thought about pouring himself a large whisky but he continued drinking water as he found a series of speeches and quotes by the self-proclaimed "man of the people". It was often the case that the more the assassin knew about his target the more he judged that they deserved to die. *But that might be the case with everyone*, Devlin grimly half-joked.

"Inequality is unnatural. All property is theft. The state is a tool to compel people to live in harmony... I care about the NHS more deeply than anything in the world. It is our oldest, greatest institution. Despite these recent stories about abuse, corruption, waste and unlawful killings, it is still the best health service in the world. Every staff member, especially the migrant workers, should be given a badge with "angel" written upon it... We must live within our means, even if we need to borrow money to do so... Because of the courage and goodness of the IRA we now have a peace process... I believe in trade unionism, social justice and nationalising the railways. That's my religion. And I want my congregation to be the entire country... This is not a time for self-aggrandisement, but Vision is my vision... Have you been to

Cuba? Well, I have. And everyone in Havana walks around with a smile on their face. If Fidel Castro was a dictator, he was a benign one - who cared about his country as much as I care about mine... There are times when I can sympathise with the caliphate. America is Satan... Providing all-female carriages on our trains is the most important issue dominating my time at the moment. It's not segregation, it's emancipation. Why? Because I say so... Price and wage fixing, high taxation and five-year plans can work. If you just have the vision, pardon the pun. If you just have hope."

Devlin reacted with amusement, boredom and worry at different junctures during his browsing. Eventually tiredness started to get the better of him – and Violet deserved his attention, far more than Ewan Slater. But he didn't want to succumb to sleep quite yet. He had a proper drink – and then another – before having a cold shower. Devlin closed his eyes and imagined the water washing his sins and troubles away. The plughole burped, with satisfaction, as it swallowed them down. But as Devlin opened his eyes he knew that there were some sins that could never be washed away. Or forgiven.

10.

Porter removed his reading glasses and pinched the bridge of his nose. It was late. His head ached. His stomach rumbled. But there was still work to be done. He put his glasses back on, drained what coffee was left in his cup and continued to read the intelligence reports on Mason Talbot that Mariner had sent over in a secure file. He just needed one nugget of evidence or information to use as leverage against the American. He needed some "treasure", as George Smiley might have called it, Porter wistfully thought. He searched in vain however for a compromising link between Talbot and Ewan Slater. He was even tempted at one point to contact Slater and confront him on the issue. But it was too risky. He didn't want to just hazard a guess that there was a connection between the two men.

Porter had spent most of the night reviewing the agent's career and profile. Searching for a chink in his enemy's armour. He was unsurprised to discover that, before his posting in London, Talbot had worked in Iraq, overseeing the set-up of "Camp Redemption" at Abu Ghraib. He had also been involved in several of cases of rendition. Porter noted how late amendments to the reports stated categorically that Jack Straw and David Miliband had no knowledge of any of the operations Talbot and his agents participated in.

Porter recalled the paddle-shaped scanner again Cutter used to check for electronic devices. It reminded him of the wooden paddle his Housemaster had used on him at school, years ago. The fixer wasn't prone to violent thoughts, but he felt an urge to throttle Talbot with the scanner (or his old Housemaster's bat) when he was at the house in Boston Place.

As Porter reviewed Mason's character and career he felt a nagging sense of shame, as well as revilement, as he noticed parallels between himself and the American agent. Had he not blackmailed people in the past and exploited assets to secure his objectives? Had he not acted as a middle-man in carrying out numerous contract killings? Porter had as much blood on his hands as anyone. The words "charming", "cultured" and "ruthless" were employed to describe the American. The same words had been used to describe Porter.

He glanced at the family photo next to his computer and felt an invisible blow to his solar plexus, winding him, as he imagined what would happen if he defied Talbot. The story might make the tabloids, as well as the broadsheets. The summer party invites would dry up, although he would be attending in spirit as a central topic of conversation, no doubt. His clubs would revoke his membership, although not all of them. Some would still be happy to take his money. It would be difficult, after all, for him to show his face at an establishment whilst also serving a long prison sentence. Those who already knew about his profession – and had hired him – would act with the most pronounced shock and opprobrium, he fancied.

But Porter had experienced enough "society" to last him ten lifetimes. His wine cellar was equal to the Garrick's too. His dog Marlborough was sufficient company – and far more loyal and trustworthy than any politician or magistrate.

Porter's heart sank, however, as he thought of his family. His children would be shunned or bullied – and asked to leave their schools. Victoria's friends would turn their back and look down their noses at her (women are the fairer – and crueller – sex). She would be cast out of her church, as if she were a witch from Salem. The charities she was involved in would ask her to resign – for the good of the organisation. He would be responsible for ruining her life. Why wouldn't she leave him? Why shouldn't she leave him – and take the children? They would have to sell the house – their home. The authorities would utilise new terrorist legislation and aim to appropriate his assets.

Some of it may be considered blood money, but it's still my money.

More importantly Porter knew that, should Talbot leak information about the contract killings he oversaw, his life could be forfeit. Although he had neither ordered the hits, or pulled the trigger, the associates and the families of the victims could hold him responsible. Half his business had been generated over the years from a sense of grievance and vengeance, on the part of his clients. Nothing was sacred to them, except the need for the debt to be settled. For justice to be done. Porter believed that revenge should have some usefulness, utility, rather than just be a crime of passion. But he long ago conceded that he wasn't made like other people. His enemies would consider his family a justified target as well, to repay the debt they owed Porter. And Talbot knew that too.

The fixer found himself grinding his teeth and cursing Devlin's name. The widower had nothing to lose. Whilst the husband and father had everything to lose. But he breathed out and quickly forgave his friend. Devlin wasn't the enemy. Talbot was.

All was not lost, Porter told himself in a feeble fit of logic or optimism. Mariner had messaged to say that he was still digging up information on the CIA operative. The fixer had called in a favour from a contact at MI6 to pass on any intelligence too. From the sigh Porter emitted – and his hollowed-out expression – all seemed lost however.

"Darling, it's getting late. Would you like me to leave you some supper out on the kitchen table?" Victoria exclaimed, from the other side of the door to his office in the garden. There was a chequered strain of fondness and falsity to her tone. She wanted to convey that everything was as normal, but she really knew that something was wrong. Her anxieties would remain bubble-wrapped and boxed-up though. A marriage can't survive without its secrets and small – or large – deceptions.

Porter dabbed at the film of sweat across his corrugated brow with a handkerchief his wife had given to him on his last birthday. He then sculptured his features into a crescent smile before opening the door.

"I'll be finished up soon, I promise," Porter remarked.

"It's a beautiful night. I may stay up and have a glass of wine on the terrace," she replied, hoping to further coax her husband outside.

It was indeed a fine evening. The stars seemed as polished as the buttons on his dress uniform. The sky was a glossy sable. Birdsong threaded its way through the hedgerows and trees. Lilting, lulling – as opposed to just loud.

"It is beautiful." Porter agreed, without really noticing or caring.

Yet he thought to himself how his wife was beautiful and a welcome sight. Her skin was bronzed, but as soft as velvet. She wore a simple floral-print dress which fluttered in the breeze and yet quite rightly also wanted to cling to her elegant figure. He caught the scent of her shampoo in the air and breathed it in. He tried to identify the constituent parts of the whole: cinnamon, jasmine, coconut, lemon. Porter increasingly thought how much older than his wife he must now look, but took consolation from the fact that no matter how old he got she would make him feel younger. The former officer knew that some people thought him as dry as piece of flat-bread. But with Victoria he could be romantic – and even sentimental. Porter didn't much care if others considered him cold or stuffy – because he knew that she knew the truth.

Porter would ultimately beat Talbot, he vowed. Because he had something worth fighting for.

11.

Morning. The city was shrouded in a dirty grey mist, as if everyone had been chain smoking since dawn. A watery, jaundiced light eventually seeped through, like puss secreting from a wound.

Devlin pretended to be a friend of Kylie's brother. He composed a short note, enclosed with ten thousand pounds (which he retrieved from his bug-out bag at the bottom of his wardrobe), explaining how Kylie could use the money to pay back her brother's debt. She should then use any money left over to help pay for the wedding.

He checked for a tail - and ran a few counter-surveillance moves for good measure – before heading over to the barmaid's flat and posting the letter and money through her door.

As Devlin walked home he sketched out a schedule for the day ahead. After taking Violet for a walk he would vacate the flat, before Emma was due to turn up, and visit Bob at the care home. After a couple of drinks in the pub he would then visit Holly's grave. Once back home he would check-in with Oliver and run-through the plan for tomorrow.

Devlin's schedule – and innards – span out of kilter however as he opened the door to find Emma already in his apartment, wrestling Violet for possession of a plastic bone.

He briefly stood dumbstruck, or enamoured. His mouth fell open, forming a perfect O – as if he were a goldfish. He was a little shocked – as opposed to angry – that Emma had turned up so early and let herself in. Indeed, he quickly realised how pleased he was to see her. There was a surprising lack of awkwardness. Maybe it was her calm and heartfelt smile, putting him at ease.

"I'm sorry, I know I'm early. I hope you don't mind that I let myself in. I was lucky with the traffic," she warmly remarked, crimsoning a little. Emma hoped Devlin would believe that she had arrived early by accident, rather than design.

"No, it's fine. I'm not the only one who's pleased to see you it seems," Devlin suggested, nodding towards to an ebullient Violet. The stupidly happy mongrel wagged her tail and excitedly paced up and down. Her claws made tap dancing sounds upon the wooden floor. The animal constantly alternated her gaze between Devlin and Emma – perhaps hoping that Emma had come back to live with them again. Devlin was reminded of the enormity of Emma's selfless act, to let Violet stay with him after they separated. It was probably the nicest thing anyone had ever done for him.

The first thing he noticed about Emma was how she had grown her hair long. Her fire-red tresses seemed to burn brighter, and cascaded down to her breasts. Her freckles were in bloom too, as they had been last summer. What little make-up she wore complimented her prettiness. Her lips were the colour of strawberry ice-cream, as opposed to strawberries. Her eyes were neither alluring nor demure. But her eyes were attractive and striking because they were kind.

Emma had given herself an extra spray of her favourite perfume that morning. She was wearing a cream, A-line thigh-high summer dress, belted at the waist to accentuate her figure. She had only bought the outfit, in *House of Fraser*, two days ago, along with the dark blue strappy heels she had on. Devlin thought how she was probably due to have a meeting, or attend an event later. He was too tired, modest or innocent to think how Emma had dressed-up to impress him. Whether consciously or unconsciously she still wanted him to find her attractive still - or show Devlin how she was flourishing without him. But not from a motivation of spite.

"I was about to take Violet for a walk. Would you like to join us?"

"I'd love to."

The heavy cloud cover lifted like a curtain in a theatre, to a musical – and the sun came out. Small waves slapped against the bank of the Thames, as the pleasure boats began to cruise along the moss-green river.

Anyone might have mistaken Devlin and Emma for a newly married couple as they walked their dog, chatted and laughed together.

At first, upon seeing Devlin, Emma thought he had changed. And not for the better. He appeared tired, defeated, like a man twice his age. He was, for him, out of shape and a little overweight. His t-shirt needed tucking in and his hair was slightly unkempt. His eyes were dark, almost bruised, from sleeplessness or drink. His voice seemed rougher. Yet essentially Devlin was still the same, she realised. Melancholy. Dry-witted. His face – being – was still a swirling, cracked mosaic of strength and vulnerability. He still needed saving.

"And how's your mum?" Devlin asked, as they caught-up with various things.

"Oh, she's still her usual, unbearable self. She might even have a nervous breakdown one day, instead of just always being on the cusp of one. My dad should be given a medal for putting up with her. Although I'm sure he'd prefer just to lower his golf handicap."

Emma failed to mention how her mum disapproved of her fiancé, Jason. During their first lunch together she had asked her daughter's new suitor if he was Catholic. He wasn't. God was a "cultural construct" for the tax lawyer.

"I can accept that someone called Jesus Christ existed. I just think he was a carpenter rather than the son of God," Jason asserted.

"He's an atheist," she had said, with some alarm, after the boyfriend left. "It could be worse though, I suppose. He could be C of E," she added, without a hint of humour – which was what made it funnier for Emma and her long-suffering father.

"Daddy misses you, of course," Emma remarked to Devlin, just after throwing another biscuit up in the air and having Violet catch it in her mouth. "He talks about you as if you were a fish. The one that got away. He's got no one in his life now to chat about military history with... How's Bob?"

"Unfortunately, he's gone downhill since Mary passed away. He can't really hold a conversation anymore. He gets confused. He barely eats... And he cries when he remembers Mary. He just lays in bed most of the time with the TV on, although he can't really take things in. The easiest way to describe it is that he seldom laughs or smiles anymore."

Devlin mumbled rather than spoke – and for the first time since Emma had known him the ex-soldier looked like he was going to break down and cry. He felt buffeted and burdened, plagued by the harpies of grief, guilt and Mason Talbot. Everything invisibly attacked him at once and the combatant couldn't fight back. His features crumbled in on themselves like a crushed polystyrene cup. Her heart went out to him, as did her fingertips as she gently placed her hand upon his arm. Devlin realised just how much he needed the touch, once he felt it.

"You must be glad you've found someone else, given the state I'm in?" Devlin joked, doing his best to raise a smile.

Emma nearly answered "no".

"I'm sorry," he then said, simply and sincerely.

"That's okay, don't be silly. You have been through a lot recently, what with Bob's dementia and Mary passing away."

"No, I mean I'm sorry – for everything. For hurting you. I wanted to be the man you wanted me to be. But couldn't. I regret how I treated you – and how things ended – but I don't regret getting to know you. Being with you, Emma."

Tears glistened in her eyes. She had rehearsed what she wanted to say to Devlin, if she encountered such a scene, so many times. But silence seemed apt. If he would have asked her to keep him company all day – and all night – she probably would have said yes. They both leaned towards each other, as they sat on the bench. Propping each other up. Emma squeezed his hand. Devlin was responsive and squeezed hers in return. Their heartbeats and breathing synchronised.

"I hope you're happy now," Devlin said, his voice still a little broken.

"I am," Emma replied, lying. She increasingly preferred to spend time by herself, rather than be in Jason's company. She told herself that this didn't matter. But it did. He was a junior partner at a law firm in Holborn. He still had a lot to prove, to himself, his successful father and the partnership. Every discussion – or argument – between them was akin to a small court case. And he needed to win it, either through semantics or plea bargaining. He felt lucky to have her – and Jason loved the woman he asked to marry – but Emma sometimes felt she was little more than an adornment, a piece of eye candy who could hold an intelligent conversation around a dinner table with clients and associates. But he was decent and stable. And Emma wanted to marry him, she told herself – although her decision was slightly coloured by a desire to have children. At least he had never been married before. All the time, when Emma had lived with Devlin, she felt like she had been competing with the ghost of his first wife – and she could never live up to Holly. She was sacred. Perfect. Yet Emma missed how Devlin would put her first when they were making love. Jason couldn't compete with her first love in that respect, either from a lack of technique or selflessness.

"I know that other people say how they'd like to remain friends, but I would. I've enjoyed this morning, despite me just making a fool of myself and doubtless depressing you. But not many people I know can hold their drink like you, or have read Graham Greene. It'd be a shame to lose you altogether."

Emma smiled and the tears began to glisten in her eyes for a different reason.

"I'd like to see you again too. Not many people can put up with me complaining about by mum. And I've got no one to discuss Graham Greene – and, of course, Jane Austen - with as well. And I've missed Violet," she remarked. At the sound of her name the dog jumped up and Emma let her lick her face.

She was tempted to mention, either casually or more seriously, how much she missed Devlin. But she didn't. Yet.

"What's the form on an old boyfriend buying a present for his ex for her wedding day?"

"How about you just take care of yourself? That can be your gift to me.'"I'd much prefer to buy you a microwave or fridge freezer. It'll be a lot easier for me, than taking care of myself," Devlin said, with a piratical grin.

Emma laughed, albeit underneath she still worried about the lapsed Catholic – and wanted to save him.

12.

Devlin and Emma decided to have lunch together in one of their favourite restaurants, overlooking the river. As they parted, after their meal, Emma kissed him on the cheek and embraced Devlin, in more than just a casual fashion, before finally saying goodbye. Both Devlin and Violet gazed longingly at Emma, as her heels sounded across the wooden decking and the breeze played with lose strands of her silken red hair. Devlin sighed and then breathed in her perfume, as if he was doing so one last time.

The next notable smell to prickle Devlin's nostrils was that of the mix of bleach, lavender and cauliflower cheese – when he entered the foyer of the care home. Despite the bright décor of the home a sense of joy could only be a fleeting visitor, rather than permanent resident, in the building. Even the plastic flowers, located on the desk at the main reception, seemed to be withering, Devlin fancied.

He headed upstairs to Bob's room, passing other residents along the way. Most sat calmly and quietly in God's waiting room, gently rocking or talking to themselves. Yet a few still had a glint in their eye – a divine spark - and smiled and said hello to the familiar face.

Devlin forced a smile onto his careworn countenance and greeted his foster parent. Bob Woodward appeared both decrepit and child-like at the same time. His rheumy eyes peered out at the world with a blend of innocence, vacancy, disorientation and sorrow. The aged, dementia sufferer reminded Devlin of photographs of WW2 prisoners of war, which he had seen as a teenager. Bob was wearing chocolate brown trousers, a flannel shirt and corduroy slippers. Most of his clothes were now too big for him, due to his recent weight loss. What little hair he had left was cobweb-grey. His liver-spotted hands loosely held a remote control and banana skin. White, wiry hairs hung down from his chin, similar to a Billy goat. Certainly, he could be as gruff as a Billy goat on occasion, Devlin thought to himself. Bob was sitting in a wheelchair, as the nurse advised that the frail patient was too weak to walk unaided and unaccompanied now.

"Would you like to come out to the garden and have a cigarette?" Devlin asked, akin to a father encouraging his son to do something.

"Okay," Bob replied, croakily, whilst nodding his head. Devlin took consolation from the flicker of recognition and desire in the old man's expression.

The air was awash with buttery sunshine. Ferns, yuccas and rosebushes bordered the tennis court-sized garden. Devlin politely – even cheerfully – greeted the staff and other residents enjoying the clement weather. He wheeled Bob next to a beechwood table on the lawn, with a parasol over it providing some shade. His pale face it up in conjunction with Devlin lighting his cigarette for him. As well as retrieving his cigarettes from the top of the wardrobe in Bob's room he had also picked up a steel hipflask, containing a measure or two of navy rum. Devlin poured out the elixir into a glass for the former merchant seaman.

"You're a good boy," his father said, lovingly.

Devlin's face creased-up and for a moment he was caught, betwixt and between, smiling and sobbing. He couldn't quite decide if life was a comedy or a tragedy. If it was a comedy, that was sad. If a tragedy, you had to laugh. Devlin was grateful for the kind words – and happy at witnessing Bob's contented expression. But tears welled in Devlin's eye because he knew just how much he hadn't been "a good boy".

After a few drags on his cigarette – and a couple of sips of rum – something seemed to click into place inside of Bob's brain and he spoke with purpose and feeling:

"I know I'm turning into a silly sod. I keep falling asleep and talk all sorts of bollocks. I keep forgetting things too. But I don't want you to forget how proud your mother and I are of you."

The lump in Devlin's throat prevented him from replying.

"And how's that nice girlfriend of yours, Gemma?" Bob added.

"She's fine. We had lunch together today."

"Good, good," the old man said, whilst nodding and gazing off into the distance, the cigarette burning itself down to the butt.

Devlin thought how his foster-dad still, just about, resembled Michael Caine. He had looked and sounded like the cockney actor most of his life – and even wore similar glasses. It had been just after watching *Zulu* when Devlin had mentioned his intention of joining the army. Bob neither encouraged nor discouraged his son in his decision.

"You're a man now. It's your choice. Just don't go getting shot, otherwise you mother will kill you. And me too."

Devlin looked back fondly on the afternoons they had spent together, fishing, drinking down the pub or watching football (because the "poxy commentators" often got on his nerves Bob would watch the matches with the sound off – and listen to Neil Diamond, The Drifters or Frank Sinatra instead). Devlin also remembered how Bob had introduced him to John Buchan, having given the teenager a copy of *The Thirty-Nine Steps* one summer. Perhaps the book led him down his path. In which case, Devlin didn't know whether to blame or thank Bob. He missed Mary. And he missed Bob, even though he was still alive and saw him every week. But dementia had eaten away at his humour and dignity. The postman had been honest and hard-working, two traits which Devlin found scarce, outside of the army. He also loved his wife with an old-fashioned affection and devotion which this age was probably incapable of understanding, let alone duplicating.

Devlin was pleased that, for part of an afternoon, he had his father back with him. But ultimately a mournfulness gripped his heart as he stared at the pitiful figure. Death in life. Dementia had borrowed itself deep into his bones, like a cancer. There would be no Lazarus-like, miracle recovery. It was just about managing decline, fighting a losing battle. But it was one that had to be fought. The reward for a long life is not altogether so much of a reward, Devlin gloomily thought.

The two men largely sat in silence for the next hour. Bob issued the occasional confused utterance, or gave monosyllabic answers to Devlin when he tried to start a conversation. The weather continued to be fine though and the old man enjoyed a cold glass of milk, as well as his navy rum.

When Bob started to nod off Devlin wheeled him back upstairs and positioned him in front of the television. The son then bent down and kissed his father on his waxy forehead, before taking his leave – with tears brimming in his eyes once more.

It was getting too late now to visit the cemetery, Devlin told himself. Or perhaps he didn't want to discuss his day with Holly, given the amount of time he had spent with Emma.

During the can ride to the *Huntsman* Devlin dozed off a couple of times. He first dreamed about Bob. Devlin had come into his room at the nursing home and found him on the floor, having fallen out of his chair. Despite his emaciated figure Devlin found it a burden to pick him up. He shoulders burned, like he was back in the regiment again, carrying a backpack of bricks during basic training. Also, when he tried to place Bob back in his wheelchair the contraption kept toppling over. It was like trying to balance a bullet on its head.

The second dream was about Emma. The couple were having dinner by the hexagonal shaped swimming pool in the resort in Gambia they had holidayed at for a week. Not another soul was around, as though Devlin had booked out the entire restaurant for the night. She was wearing the two-toned Karen Millen dress which Devlin had bought for Emma before the trip. The outfit clung limpet-like to her lithe figure, yet could fall from her body like silk. He wanted to tell her how much he wanted her but his mouth was sown shut. His feet were nailed to the floor, preventing him from going to her. Or kneeling before her, either in the act of proposing or pleasuring her. Or supplicating her, to ask for forgiveness. Her lips were moist with champagne. Emma was equally desirous and desirable.

"I want to tell you something," she part teased, part prepared to confess.

Devlin wondered if she was going to ask if he would marry her, or tell him how much she wanted him - or reveal she was pregnant.

But before Emma could say anything else the taxi braked sharply, as it pulled up outside the pub.

Terry poured Devlin a pint before he even entered, having spotted his friend through the window, paying the cab driver. As he got to the bar Alan and James, the couple who lived next door to the pub, were having a discussion cum argument about whether to attend a Star Trek or Star Wars convention later in the year.

"Terry, we're never going to agree about this so why don't you decide for us?" Alan proposed, keen to settle things either way, if only because he wanted to go outside and smoke another cigarette.

"That's a good idea. Which is a first for Alan," James replied, only half-jokingly. "What do you think, Terry?"

"Well, having listened to you both for the past half an hour I can honestly say that I genuinely – and passionately – couldn't care less about which conference you go to," the landlord jovially exclaimed.

Alan and James grinned and nodded in sympathy, whilst "Welsh Mick", another regular, let out a cackle and tapped his silver-handled walking stick on the floor a few times as a form of applause. Mick, a former Royal Engineer, had the uncanny ability to vent bile and get upset about any and everything in the world – but then, aided and abetted by a couple of ciders, he would then duly laugh at any and everything happening in the world.

Devlin got a round in for the group of friends at the bar and, for a blessed hour or so, he was able to drink a measure from Lethe's cup and forget about Bob, Emma, Holly and the job he would have to do the next day. The tension in his shoulders dissipated, like an aspirin dissolving in water. He laughed out loud several times and took an interest in the lives of his drinking companions. But he knew he would have to drink again from the river Acheron, sooner rather than later. Despite the protestations of Terry and the regulars Devlin excused himself after only a few drinks. He needed to return home with a clear head and contact Porter. The two men, employing coded phrases, confirmed arrangements for the next day.

For better or worse, Ewan Slater was as good as dead.

13.

A fleet of battleship-grey clouds anchored itself in the sky. The rain pelted and hissed. Relentlessly. *Perfect weather for killing*, Devlin drily posed. People kept their heads down in such weather, oblivious to what was going on around them. The only thing they were concerned about was getting out of the rain. Even more usually he would travel about in the capital, unnoticed. Devlin rifled through a cupboard and retrieved his large, black, Fulton umbrella. Porter would no doubt carry his own umbrella – and both men would be able to shield themselves from London's prying CCTV cameras.

Devlin woke-up early that morning. After showering and dressing in some black jeans and a plain blue shirt he smoked a couple of cigarettes and drank a cup of strong coffee. He was wired, but not too much. A small element of edginess was fine, natural. He walked Violet and chatted to a couple of other dog owners he knew. They spoke about the weather and he feigned interest in their plans for the weekend ahead. All the while Devlin imagined himself taking the shot. The rain would not change anything. The room he would shoot from would provide sufficient cover. The trajectory was fine. The distance was relatively short, compared to other shots he had taken over the years, and he had no need to factor in bullet drift or the Coriolis effect.

Cutter sent a message from a burner phone, reminding him of their rendezvous. Should Devlin somehow be running late, he should let the CIA agent know immediately.

He took the tube to Baker St. Rain fell down the cheeks of the sullen, harassed passengers like teardrops. Devlin gently tapped his wedding ring against the wooden handle of his umbrella, either nervously or impatiently. A couple of hipsters blamed the summer rain on climate change (if they could they would have blamed Brexit). Devlin wryly smiled to himself as he recalled the afternoon before, in the *Huntsman*. Someone, a newcomer to the pub, asked if he was a climate change denier.

"It's not that I don't think climate change exists, it's just that I don't care about it," Devlin responded, with a nonchalant shrug of his shoulders.

The regulars laughed, much to the chagrin of the po-faced stranger.

The contract killer shook the incident out of his mind, like a forester macheting his way through the jungle, and thought about the vehicle Porter would arrange for them. Like the fixer himself, the car would be practical, reliable and modest. Danny Tanner could be trusted to dispose of the vehicle too. Porter met the former Royal Engineer during his time in the army. If Tanner liked you – and your money was good – he was a useful and loyal associate. The rest of the world however was fair game to fleece. Tanner owned a string of garages across London which, by day, also served as chop shops. Occasionally, at night, the upstairs offices of the garages doubled-up as pop-up poker bars, replete with serving girls and mixologists. And cocaine, of course, which only the house was permitted to sell.

The heavens continued to open as Devlin came out the station, not that he believed that God was ever on his side. He met with Porter on the corner of Glentworth St. He nearly didn't recognise the former Guards officer, such was his casual dress. He looked like a plumber. Devlin had never seen Porter wear jeans before, or indeed anything with a Nike swoosh emblazoned across it. Casual, for Porter, usually meant leaving the house without wearing a tie or pocket square. The two men nodded at one another, beneath their umbrellas.

"Nice weather for it," Porter drolly remarked, although like his associate he was all too aware of the benefits from the persistent showers.

"We know more than most how it never rains but it pours," Devlin replied, smiling lightly as he noticed how his friend had swapped his Patek Philippe, for a digital Casio watch, for the day.

As the pair walked towards Boston Place Porter made small talk by asking if Emma had come over to his flat the previous day. Devlin answered that she had, but failed to mention they had spoken and had lunch. Perhaps he would say something at the end of the week, after he processed how he – and she – felt.

They were met at the door to the house in Boston Place by the American who had followed Devlin into the *Huntsman*, a few of days ago. They were then led upstairs, where Cutter was waiting for them. He had taken his jacket off, revealing his gun and solid torso. His build and square head made him look like a turret.

"Is Mason not going to grace us with his presence today?" Porter queried, noting his absence.

"Mr. Talbot is attending an important meeting elsewhere," Cutter flintily replied, conveying his dislike for English irony and sarcasm.

Plausible deniability, Porter thought to himself.

Cutter got down to business straightaway, keen for everyone to be ahead of schedule. He unceremoniously pulled out a British Army issue L115A3 sniper's rifle, complete with adjustable bipod, an all-weather telescopic sight and suppressor. Cutter also handed over a 5-round box of 8.59mm bullets.

Cutter issued the asset with an equally untraceable Sig Sauer P226 – with shoulder holster, magazine and suppressor. Devlin squeezed the guard of the pistol more than he needed to, as if giving a firm handshake to an old friend.

The American invited Devlin to check the weapons and ammunition. He disassembled and reassembled the rifle on the kitchen table. Once Cutter saw that the Englishman was satisfied he ran through the plan, again. His voice was hard, galvanised. His thoughts and speech worked in straight lines. At any moment Porter fancied Cutter might revert to being a marine and start bellowing orders, or shout "Oorah" as a stirring refrain.

"We will drive you to Shelley St, a couple of streets away from where your vehicle is located, on Derwent Row. You will then drive to the house on Cooper Rd. We currently have a car parked outside, which we will remove just before you arrive. The property is empty – but I have posted a man in line of sight of the address, just in case someone attempts to knock at the door or loiters outside when you enter or exit the address. The second-floor back bedroom to the house looks out onto Lewis St and the front of Hayden Mole's home. You have been given photographs, maps and diagrams of the address – and the surrounding area. Mole is our target's campaign manager. Ewan Slater has set aside the afternoon to conduct meetings in the office on the ground floor of the house. At precisely 14.00 a call will come through to the office. Slater will be asked to come to the phone, which is situated by the window. You will be able to clearly see his silhouette. The phone is an old-fashioned one, connected by a wire, so the target will remain in view for a required period of time. Once I give the order you will take the shot. Failure if not an option. Even if you claim that the rifle has misfired, or the shot goes amiss, I will expect you to draw your pistol and fire a cluster of rounds at the target. Your marksmanship is at a standard to do so. We will leave it to you to ensure that you do not leave any evidence in the room. You are responsible for your own extraction. Do not attempt to contact us after the operation. We will contact you in our own time... Any questions?"

The personal bled into the professional after Cutter's debriefing, as the CIA operative smirked-cum-sneered at Devlin. Cutter wanted him to know that he was the master – and the trigger man was the dog. He wanted to posit that the marine was superior to the squaddie, the lawman was superior to the criminal – and the American was superior to the Englishman. There had been moments when Cutter had sized up his counterpart – and wondered about the extent of his training and number of kills to his name. Unlike many of the other assets Talbot was responsible for running Cutter was curious, or frustrated, in regards to knowing what made the ex-soldier tick. Devlin had the air of a wild horse, who still wouldn't let anyone ride him. He needed to be broken.

"Don't worry, this will all soon be over and you will be able to go back to your old life – or what little life you appear to have. You can spend your days drinking again," Cutter remarked, unable or unwilling to disguise his animosity towards Devlin.

"As Sinatra once said, "I feel sorry for people that don't drink, because when they wake up in the morning, that is the best they are going to feel all day.""

Devlin internally doffed his cap to Bob Woodward, for sharing the quote with him many years ago.

Cutter sneered again, like he was looking at a failed recruit, and shook his head disapprovingly. Reprovingly.

"You have no code, no honour. You fight for nothing. Or for a few measly bucks. You're half the man you once were, since leaving the army, I imagine."

"Be all you can be. Isn't that the mantra of the marine corps? If you're not being all that you can be now, you might want to go back for some basic training. But should you be being all you can be at the moment then your life may be considered just as tragic as mine," Devlin said, the corner of his mouth raised in a smile. Rather than treating the American with contempt, Devlin wanted to convey how much Cutter amused him – which only riled and antagonised the agent even more.

"You don't want to make an enemy of me," Cutter threatened, approaching the Englishman and puffing out his chest. Eyeballing him. His breath smelled of gum and cranberry juice.

"It might prove preferable to having you as a friend," Devlin wryly, unflinchingly replied.

Cutter initially screwed up his features in disdain but then forced a smile. He didn't want to give his opponent the satisfaction of seeing him losing control or reveal or any weak spots.

And they still had a job to do.

14.

Porter glanced at Devlin, out the corner of his eye, and noticed the look of concentration or concern on the assassin's face. He quickly shifted his focus back to the road however as Porter drove the car through the streets of Islington and switched the windscreen wipers to on to intermittent. The fixer wasn't quite sure if the silence between the two men was comfortable or eerie. He offered up a brief prayer to God, or the cosmos, or Good Luck, that they would come through the day unscathed. Porter justly understood however that his prayers to God might fall on deaf ears, for assorted reasons.

Devlin lowered his window and allowed a blast of fresh air to revitalise his skin. A thick, soupy humidity accompanied the rain. He had overheard two people on the tube earlier describe the heat as "oppressive" and "unbearable". Devlin recalled the heat in Afghanistan, which could sap a man's strength and will to live. The sun would hang upon the shoulders like a set of stocks and cook you in your body armour. Sticky, salty sweat poured down faces like rain. One needed to constantly gulp down water, like a camel stopping off at a wadi.

The heat and humidity would not bother him. He could kill in all weathers. But something did begin to bother him – a gadfly buzzing around in his head - although he couldn't quite put his finger on what it was. Devlin compressed his jaw and re-focused on the task at hand. He castigated himself a little for forgetting to bring a small towel, which he liked to place between his shoulder and the rifle stock. He wondered if the recoil of the weapon would feel familiar or alien to him. It had been eighteen months or so since he had fired a L115A3. Cutter had offered to arrange a practise session for Devlin, to re-introduce him to the weapon, but he declined. Had he done so out of pride or arrogance? Normally he would have been meticulous in his preparation. The harder you practise the luckier you get. Train hard, fight easy. Due to the time frame and parameters of the job however Devlin hadn't reconnoitred the target or location properly. He was just being asked – or rather ordered – to point and shoot.

"We're here," Porter announced, as he turned into Cooper Rd. The road was lined with terrace houses. Most had been split up into flats, some were still council properties - and some were homes to middle-class families, with two cars, a Filipino nanny and a Somalian cleaner. As Cutter had promised, the parking space, directly outside the property, was free. The agent had provided Porter with a tracker and radio after the debrief.

Both men put up their umbrellas after getting out the non-descript vehicle. Should any neighbours have noted the two figures they were unable to catch a proper view of their faces. Porter retrieved the rod bag from the backseat whilst Devlin carried a fishing tackle holdall containing latex gloves, hairnets and his Sig Sauer pistol. Without appearing to be overly rushing they quickly entered the empty property.

The two men put on their latex gloves and hairnets. They had no desire to leave any trace evidence. Porter had considered putting plastic coverings over their shoes but he had instructed Tanner to destroy all their garments, when disposing of the car and weapons, and provide new clothes at their drop-off point.

The musty-smelling house was half-furnished with bits of old furniture and worn carpets. A film of coarse dust and dirt covered the stairs and surfaces. Mouse droppings and cobwebs decorated skirting boards and crevices. The property was due to be sold in September.

Without a word said Porter and Devlin ascended the stairs. Onwards and upwards. Porter briefly comforted himself with the thought that he would be carrying his own rod bag tomorrow, fly-fishing on the banks of the Kennett. He looked forward to emptying his mind, or filling it with plans of getting out from under Talbot's influence. The American had of course promised that their association would end after today, but he would rather trust a Turk, or Tory, than the CIA agent.

The back bedroom contained a metal-framed single-bed, a table by the window and a pine tallboy, housing a chipped figurine of a racehorse and jockey. The floral wallpaper was yellowing and peeling off in places, due to damp, and several of the wooden floorboards were warped. Motes of dust hung in the air like a congregation of flies over a mound of garbage.

A dull light crawled through the window, which was half covered by a new bark-brown roller blind (which Cutter's people had recently fitted). Both men surveyed the scene. Either through luck or judgement Cutter had picked a favourable spot. Hayden Mole's house was directly opposite. Beneath them resided a row of backyards but the rain ensured that no one was sitting out in them. In between the yards – and Mole's terrace house – was Lewis St, containing a few parked cars. Recently painted iron railings stood at the front of Mole's home. To the right of its red door was the large window to his office. Devlin and Porter could already observe a couple of figures moving about, behind the net curtains.

Mole, an avowed Marxist and "fan" of the Stasi, had arranged a slew of meetings for his leader. Some related to press interviews, some to campaign funding and others to introduce Slater to people of potential influence (who they could buy, or be bought by). Porter was already familiar with Mole. A mockney accent disguised Mole's heritage of being educated at Stowe and Balliol College. He was the son of Tarquin Mole, former head of programming for Radio Four. Mole worked as a Fleet Street journalist for a decade or so, before becoming a senior press officer for the National Union of Miners in the mid-eighties (during which time he accused the SAS of assassinating half a dozen of its members). After resigning from his position at the NUM (his justification being that they were neither militant nor radical enough for him) Mole went back to being a political commentator, although his reputation was tarnished when he was caught falsifying evidence for a story. His long-term mentor and ally – Ewan Slater – quickly hired him as Vision's Director of Strategy and Communications. Mole described himself in his recent autobiography, "Left Standing", as a cross between Alastair

Campbell and Gerry Adams – as though such a creature should be lauded and admired. Should Devlin's bullet somehow travel through his target today – and fell Mole too – then Porter promised himself he would drink two large brandies that evening, instead of just one.

Whilst Devlin pulled down the blind fully and commenced to assemble his weapon Porter paced up and down the room, craving a cigar. This was the first time he had accompanied an associate on a job. Usually he was miles away. Plausible deniability. Although Porter was slightly anxious, he was in no mood to panic. Because of his time as a Guards officer (or other regiments might joke that despite his time in the Guards) Porter was no stranger to gunfire or death. Although he hadn't pulled the trigger himself, he was aware of how much blood he had on his hands in relation to previous contract killings too. But it would soon all be over, the fixer told himself. Porter also took heart from seeing Devlin in action. The ex-soldier was a picture of determination and professionalism as he methodically attached the bipod, suppressor, telescopic sight and magazine to the tried and tested L115A3. He was akin to an artist, readying his easel. More than anyone else he knew, Devlin could be relied upon to get the job done.

Cutter's stentorian voice came over the radio. It was 13.50.

Devlin pulled the blind and window up to the required height. The rifle's bipod rested on an oblong table. Devlin was standing, directing the weapon downwards. His features were neither relaxed nor tense. The barrel of the weapon remained inside the room. The butt was nestled comfortably in his shoulder. With his free hand, Devlin adjusted the telescopic sights. The ground-floor window loomed even larger in front of him. He closed the blind and informed Cutter that he would be in position at 13.58.

Devlin waited, as patient as a priest – waiting for his flock to arrive. Or for someone to enter his confessional. But beneath his calm, focused exterior the gadfly still unsettled him. He remembered the last time he fired the sniper rifle. He had assassinated Dermot Cahill, the IRA brigade commander. It had been a righteous kill. George and Byron Parker, Rameen

Jamal and Faisal Ahmadi. The world was better off without them and Devlin hadn't lost any sleep over their deaths. But would the world be better off without Ewan Slater? Probably. But it was too late now to worry about breaking the sixth commandment. His own voice, or that of a devil, chimed in his ears:

Thou shalt kill.

The philosophical assassin could have argued that, had he not taken out some of his targets, then his homicidal and tyrannical victims would have caused more death and suffering than he ever could.

Devlin briefly wondered that, if he looked in a mirror right now, would he see a vile and atrophied figure? Or, in his latex gloves and hair net, would he resemble a clown more? One to be laughed at, or pitied.

If only Talbot was the target. The bullet would have been worth its weight in gold.

It was time. Cutter's voice crackled on the radio again.

Porter pulled the blind up and Devlin readied himself. The butt was buried in his shoulder once more. His index finger rested on the trigger guard. Devlin briefly closed his eyes and regulated his breathing and heartrate. He bent his knees slightly – but owned the strength and technique to hold the slightly unnatural pose. The ground floor window loomed large in the telescopic sight again. If the gadfly was still buzzing in his ear then Devlin was besting it, ignoring it. Swotting it.

The world would continue to spin on its axis should Ewan Slater perish (he should have died hereafter, Devlin thought, misquoting a line from Macbeth). Nature would be indifferent to his death and – as some believed that God was Nature – then God would not condemn the act either. Ewan Slater would trend on social media for twenty-four hours or so but then that would be it. He would be history. Or not even that. Although his wife would doubtless want to sign a book deal and carry on the mantle of his campaigning work. The world would still have its Vision.

14.00.

Devlin watched as someone came to the window and picked up the phone.

Breathe normally. Squeeze, don't pull. Keep your face close to the stock and do not jolt with the rifle.

The phone was handed to another figure – silhouette.

Cutter's incisive voice came through the radio:

"Take the shot."

The figure loomed large in the telescopic sight. Slater seemed to be facing him, presenting as big a target as possible.

The sound of the 8.59mm round leaving the weapon was a mix of a thud, a puff and a hiss. It was and it wasn't like the movies, Porter thought to himself. He watched the bullet ping through the window (which didn't smash) and the silhouette disappear from view, in the blink of an eye. It was all far less dramatic than one might have imagined, the fixer posited. Life doesn't end with a bang. But rather with a whisper. Whimper.

Whilst Porter pulled down the window and blind Devlin commenced to place the rifle back into the rod bag, after having pocketed the shell casing from the floor. They briskly – but not too hastily – descended the stairs. After taking a breath, they removed their hairnets and gloves – and then opened the front door, wiping any prints away as they did so. The police would work out that somebody had used the empty property to take the shot but the trail would end there.

Umbrellas went up. Car doors were opened. Bags were put inside. They drove away. Job done.

15.

A sombre silence hung in the air, as did a pall of cigarette smoke, as Porter drove to their rendezvous point with Danny Tanner. His stomach churned. He didn't know if he was famished, or if he wanted to be sick. He swallowed a couple of times, his Adam's apple moving up and down like a boat bobbing upon a choppy ocean. The fixer thought about saying "good job" to Devlin but it somehow felt inappropriate, or even patronising. Instead he gratefully breathed in Devlin's secondary smoke and imagined the scene back at the house. People would be confused and terrorised, fearing for their own lives. Perhaps they all rushed to the back of the property, or lay on the floor. Even – or especially – the atheists would be praying. The police and ambulance service would be called. The operator would try to urge calm from the hysterical voice on the other end of the phone. Ewan Slater would be pronounced dead. The police would scratch their heads a little, until the specialists arrived. Could they label the assassination as a right-wing terrorist attack? The BBC and press would soon descend upon the scene like vultures. They would need to cordon-off the house – and surrounding streets. Find evidence. Interview neighbours. They would be unable to set-up a security cordon around the city however, to catch the shooter. It was London. The culprits would easily be able to vanish, like Robin Hood and his Merry Men disappearing into the evergreen.

The car sloshed through another puddle. Porter glanced at Devlin. As ever his expression was inscrutable. He would have made a good poker player, albeit he probably wouldn't have much cared whether he won or lost. Or maybe Porter could read his friend. Devlin was just sad most of the time. Angry. Grieving. He was a man unwilling and unable to climb out of the hole he had dug for himself. Or he was unwilling and unable to nourish himself, like Kafka's Hunger Artist:

""I have to fast, I can't help it... I couldn't find the food I liked. If I had found it, believe me, I should have made no fuss and stuffed myself like you or anyone else.""

They arrived at the drop-off point, an empty industrial estate on the outskirts of Walthamstow. Danny Tanner was there himself to oversee things. His team were professional. Most of them were ex-army. Tanner offered the two men the use of his own car and driver.

"Just tell him where you want to go. It's all part of the service," he remarked with a wink.

The impulse to be rid of the murder weapon was, for Devlin, matched by a desire to keep the Sig Sauer pistol. As well as disposing of the rifle, vehicle and their clothes Porter also handed over the tracker and radio to be destroyed, as per Cutter's instructions. He was now free. It was job done, except for the lingering stain on his conscience. Porter wondered how many stains Talbot had on his conscience. In his mind, he might have worn them like medals – badges of honour.

Once safely ensconced in the car – and driving towards Paddington St station – Porter checked for news of the shooting on his phone. The blood drained from his tanned face as he scrolled through the various online reports. He passed the phone to Devlin. For a moment, it felt like the world had fallen off its axis. Talbot had not only blackmailed the two men, but lied to them as well – tricked them into murdering a potentially innocent man.

"Broadcaster and activist Stephen Pinner has been shot dead in Islington... Police are not ruling out a professional hit, or the crime being terror related... Pinner was shot at the home of Hayden Mole, the Director of Communications for Vision... Strictly Come Dancing's Ewan Slater was attending a meeting with Pinner at the time of the shooting."

Porter sifted through the rolodex of his mind and recalled what little he knew about the left-wing academic. He pictured his pinched features, tortoiseshell glasses, tweed suits and long, silver hair. He looked like a cross between A.C. Grayling and Charles Hawtrey. *The Observer* had called him a "British Bernie Saunders". Every week Pinner hosted a podcast which unpicked the policies and propaganda of Donald Trump's administration. He had also recently made the news by proposing a day of protest outside the new American Embassy, due to open in Battersea:

"This day will not be about me saying "no" to America, nor even about London or Britain saying "no". But the world must say "no" to Trump and his racist, bigoted and populist agenda."

Porter kept reading the ongoing reports. Pictures were emerging of journalists door-stepping the home of Pinner's wife and children. Tributes were coming in from the likes of Tariq Ali, Russell Brand and J.K. Rowling. Even Gary Lineker had sent out a tweet, condemning the heinous crime. Hayden Mole had been quick to give a comment too:

"It would come as no surprise to me if British or American intelligence agencies were found to be complicit in this murder."

For once the former hack was telling the truth, Porter mused. Although previous paranoid and unsubstantiated outbursts from Mole, during his long and un-illustrious career, meant that he had cried wolf too many times before to be listened to now. The Director of Communications was but the warm-up act for the main event, as Porter watched Ewan Slater, dressed in a tie for once, give a press conference.

"I am shocked and appalled... We must show solidarity... His day of protest should still go on, in his honour... The Labour Party treated my socialist brother as a pariah or extremist. But I was always proud to campaign and share a platform with Stephen... Hope must not give in to hate... Our meeting today was about working together more closely... Stephen was part of our family and vision..."

Porter judged how the term "political opportunist" could be considered a tautology. He put the phone back in his pocket and pensively stared out the window, engrossed in thought. As tragic as the situation might be – the turn of events provided Porter with a glimmer of hope. He hadn't been able to find any intelligence connecting Talbot to Slater because there wasn't any to find. There was every chance of finding some compromising intelligence linking Talbot to Pinner though.

All was not lost.

16.

A week after the shooting Bob Woodward passed away in his sleep. Devlin made the funeral arrangements. He had already organised a joint plot so he could be with his wife, Mary. Oliver and his family came to the service. Along with a few other people the Woodwards had taken on, as foster children over the years, Devlin gave the eulogy. His voice sometimes cracked but he stopped, drank from his glass of water, and carried on:

"...I'm not sure exactly when I started considering Bob to be my father, instead of a foster parent, but it happened. And it was a long time ago... He embodied a sense of quiet dignity, which encompassed the ability to laugh at himself... As evidenced from today I was not the only beneficiary of the Woodward's generosity, love and plain-speaking wisdom... Before he passed away Bob said to me that I was "a good boy". If I am in some way good, then credit must go to Bob and Mary. They may not have been overly concerned with the likes of climate change or the gig economy, but they did believe in courtesy and decency. The young these days are often inclined to blame society's ills on the old. I remember Bob laughing at a cartoon I showed him in *The Spectator*, shortly after the Brexit vote. It showed a row of decorated veterans on a Normandy beach, with the caption beneath, "What have old people ever done for Europe?" Young people nowadays are prone to taking pictures of themselves and looking in the mirror, but they seldom see their faults. What they believe are instances of virtue, or victimhood, are usually instances of vanity. Perhaps it's just not young people who are prone to such folly though. But nobody ever accused Bob of being vain or playing the victim. He was proud to be British and proud to be working-class. But that didn't mean he wasn't smart or well-read. One of the first memories I have of Bob is him taking me to the library and showing me the History section… And Mary was of a similar character. Except she swore less and could cook… Together they were greater than the sum of their parts. Together they could teach young people a few things about love and sacrifice – and that marriage isn't just about booking the right photographer for your wedding day… I like to think Mary was waiting for him, with a bottle of stout and shepherd's pie on the table. They are having a laugh and chinwag now, no doubt. And they would want us to do the same. Maybe she called to him in a dream, which is why he didn't want to wake up… We should celebrate his life, as opposed to just mourning and missing him."

After the funeral service and laying of the casket Devlin arranged for everyone to come back to the care home – for a party. Staff and residents were invited. A *Chas & Dave* tribute band played in the garden. Terry furnished the party with a couple of kegs of beer. Manse's Pie & Mash provided the food. Half-way through the afternoon Devlin unveiled a bench and brass plaque, in memory of Bob and Mary Woodward.

Whether due to the death of Stephen Pinner, or his father, Devlin began to drink more heavily. He ignored most of Porter's messages and turned down an invite to spend time at his house.

Terry and the regulars saw plenty of Devlin however, to the point where the landlord advised his friend that he might be drinking too much, as he helped prop him up most evenings to get him into his cab home. Mick saw Devlin's decline as no laughing matter. The old soldier knew a case of burn out when he saw it. Even Alan and James were in agreement – for once - that something was troubling their drinking companion.

Devlin desperately wanted to see Emma. Be with her. But he realised it would have been wrong and inappropriate to contact her on her honeymoon. He wanted her to be happy, more than he wanted to free himself from his own unhappiness. He thought about tracking down Helena. But what was the point?

Sleep seemed to be the only balm for his despair and depression, provided that the same ghosts who haunted his waking hours didn't occupy his dreams. Devlin began to consider sleep as the moreish bouquet, before tasting the wine of death.

He read the end chapters of Graham Greene's *The Heart of the Matter*, twice.

He stopped reading the news. The world was an awful place. He also wished to avoid seeing pictures of Pinner's wife and children on the television. Whether Pinner was wholly innocent of sin it was difficult to tell, but his family were.

The soldier often lay curled up on his sofa – or unable to get out of bed, save for walking Violet or picking up a few groceries. He'd lost his appetite for many of his favourite foods however. Devlin felt hollowed out. When he walked he felt like his body was pulling his heavy, ragged soul behind it, like a knight with his foot in the stirrups being dragged behind his horse. When he forced a smiled occasionally, out of politeness, his grin resembled a rictus. He realised that, years ago, he had given his everything to Holly. And you can't give your everything more than once. Since her death he had been playing a part in a dumb show.

For a time, just after Pinner's death, he had thought about taking out Talbot and Cutter. They deserved to die, more than most. But the switch inside of Devlin could no longer be turned on or off. He was too tired, too morose, to plan and execute another hit. The bullets could stay in the gun, for now. Although he pictured meeting Cutter in an empty, secluded car park at night. He would challenge the American to a fight. He had read-up on how the CIA agent had boxed at college and studied Krav Maga. As the two men stood in position however Devlin would remark how his opponent had brought his fists to a gunfight – and slot two into his chest in the blink of an eye.

Out of a sense of desperation, or to fuel a sense of finality, Devlin finally scratched an itch and visited the small, local Catholic church which Emma used to attend. *St Jude's*. The spire still vaunted upwards, like a spindly forearm reaching for a star, but the cross and masonry had lost its majesty. The church was a great, but doddering, thespian - who could no longer bring in the audiences. The voice may have still been soulful and sweet, but the lungs were no longer strong enough to reach even the middle aisles. Yet Devlin went in, with an age-old sense of fear and shame. The smell of damp was more prevalent than incense. He couldn't help but note how the marble font was chipped - when he dipped his fingers into the tepid holy water. Devlin felt like a child again as he devoutly closed his eyes, crossed himself and genuflected. He slowly took a turn around the church – reverently surveying his surroundings as if he were attending a museum or art exhibition. He brushed his hands along the wooden pews and marvelled at the spectacle of the stained-glass window and artistry of the stations of the cross. Although the lapsed Christian had never been to the church before the air was potent with nostalgia. The memories were so thick he needed to brush them away from his face, like flies. No matter how quietly he tried to walk his footsteps still sounded on the smooth flagstones, reminding him that God hears everything. Could the Almighty see the sinner more clearly too, now he was present in his house? Churches always brought out such conceits in him, Devlin judged.

He patiently waited in the background for someone to finish their prayer, but then approached the row of votive candles. Gleaming. Golden. Welcoming. His hand trembled and Devlin accidentally – comically - lit two candles. He found he couldn't commit to one prayer, let alone two. He placed a £50 note in the box, to compensate for his error - and walked away feeling embarrassed. And anguished, that he had forgotten how to pray and talk with God. Faith was a self-lighting candle, that Devlin had lost or thrown away some years ago. When Holly died. Or when he fulfilled his first contract for Porter.

The priest was hearing confession. He briefly remembered his old parish priest, Father Matthew. Irish. Decent. He could still smell the whisky on his breath. Devlin now realised that his rosy cheeks were caused by the burst blood vessels beneath his skin. A handful of elderly parishioners, mainly women, were sat on the front pew, waiting their turn. A couple fingered their rosary beads, in advance payment of any penance. Devlin flirted with the idea of joining them but there wouldn't be enough hours in the day for the priest to hear his sins. There were others who needed to see him - everyone was a far more deserving soul. And Devlin had no desire to be forgiven, indeed he thought how, should he go back, light a candle and pray to God – the soldier would implore the Almighty to punish him. Kill him.

The invisible weight grew too burdensome and Devlin sat on a pew, near the back of the church. The bench was more comfortable than he remembered, but the years had put some padding on his posterior he fancied. He picked up a faux-leather, dog-eared copy of the Bible from the seat in front. The pages were wafer-thin and it seemed like the book might fall apart in his hands at any moment, blow away like ashes. But it didn't.

Devlin stared at the altar after carefully putting the Bible back in its place. The musty fragrance of books and distinctive aroma of burning candles flickered in his nostrils, as welcoming as the smell of freshly baked bread. The credence table, tabernacle, ambo, chalice and baptismal font owned an air of strangeness and familiarity, piety and majesty. He was reminded of being a teenager again, sitting next to Mary Woodward. Wearing his Sunday best. Sometimes bored and sometimes struck with wonder. Shivering in Winter (and often in Spring and Autumn). Love and God sometimes in his heart.

The large crucifix naturally attracted Devlin's attention. Christ was a picture of agony and compassion. Devlin experienced an overwhelming sense of admiration and guilt in its – or His – presence - and had to turn away. Tears welled in his eyes. He missed Holly. He missed God. But they were still with him too. Just not enough. The statue was ageing but had been lovingly maintained. The blood from his wounds glistened in the candlelight from where someone had freshly painted the figure. His suffering was but a drop in the ocean compared to Christ's. Yet he seemed to be perpetually drowning from that drop in the ocean.

Devlin idly wondered if he was too Catholic or not Catholic enough to kill himself. But it didn't matter now. His mind was set. He would leave the church with an age-old sense of hope and holiness.

"Oh, that the Everlasting had not fixed His canon 'gainst self-slaughter" – he used to think.

17.

Talbot was as effusive, as he was insincere, in his apology, when he contacted Porter a fortnight after the botched – or seemingly botched – operation. Porter knew he was lying – and Talbot knew Porter knew he was lying – but form had to be preserved and the game played out. The American assured the Englishman that all debts had been paid. Ewan Slater was now his problem to deal with, alone.

"We should have lunch soon," Talbot added, hoping that just the offer of lunch would serve as sufficient goodwill.

"We should indeed. How about tomorrow? Come to the Savile. I'll reserve us a quiet table," Porter replied, a paragon of charm and generosity, having accepted Talbot's forthright apology.

"I'm not sure. I will need to check my diary," the American said, hoping the stock response would convey his lack of enthusiasm to meet.

"I insist. It'll be in your interest, as well as mine, to say yes."

There was a conscious hint of a warning, or threat, in the Englishman's voice. Porter wasn't quite altogether being the soul of politeness. Talbot knew he was hiding something – but to see his cards they would have to meet in person rather than just talk on the phone.

"I have a meeting but I can cancel it for you," the American remarked, pretending to consult his diary, when really, he flipped the pages of a sailing magazine which was to hand on his walnut desk.

Porter arrived at the Savile early, the following day. Offering to make a generous donation to the club's chosen charity – he booked out the entire first-floor terrace for the duration of lunch. Porter explained that he was hosting an important guest and needed some privacy. The manager was duly obliging but cited that, no matter how important the guest, he must abide by club rules and be dressed correctly in a jacket and tie.

Talbot, accompanied by Cutter, arrived fifteen minutes late, at 1.15. The two men squinted in the glare of cloudless summer's day as the manager led them out to their table where Porter was patiently waiting, with a glass of gin and tonic in his hand. Talbot and Porter warmly greeted one another. Both were dressed in navy blue blazers and mustard coloured corduroy trousers. Oil held their hair in place.

Talbot eyed the manila folder, beneath the salt and pepper pot, with curiosity and suspicion.

"Please, Mason, have a seat. I am afraid I am going to have to ask that we lunch alone. I have arranged for your associate to sit by the door, away from the grown-up's table," Porter said, garnishing his honeyed tone with a dash of vinegar.

Cutter's eyes bulged at the insult and the corner of his mouth subtly twitched with rage. Just as he was about to reply, or snarl, Talbot stepped in.

"I'll be fine, Vincent. Order a glass of wine. Lunch shouldn't take too long. Mr. Porter and I do not have a great deal to discuss. Our business has already been concluded."

Talbot had already decided that he would not call on his new assets to work for him again, until the dust had settled. They could have time off for good behaviour, he had joked to Cutter in the aftermath. Unless of course certain circumstances prevailed and he would need to utilise their skills again.

The former marine nodded his head. He would follow orders and not make a scene. Porter fancied that if he pursed his lips any more however they might bruise, or bleed. It was just a slight shame that Devlin couldn't be present to watch Cutter be denuded in such a fashion, Porter fancied. He had considered inviting his friend to lunch. But then re-considered. He was too unstable. Devlin might have been tempted to throw Cutter over the railings of the first-floor terrace. Management would have frowned on such behaviour.

Talbot and Porter sat in silence and perused the menu as one of the waitresses, Maria, poured the wine. Talbot covertly glanced over his menu however to take in his host. The fixer no longer seemed sheepish. Perhaps his over-confidence stemmed from being on home turf. No matter how confident the Englishman seemed though he could but bluff with the cards he'd been dealt. The American held all the aces.

"Ah, they have veal. There is no other choice. Perhaps its due to my belief that the herd are better off being kept in the dark," Talbot remarked, his cold eyes momentarily twinkling from being pleased with his own joke.

Maria took their orders and then took her leave. Once she was safely out of sight and earshot Talbot leaned forward and spoke, baring his bleached teeth a little to show his animus.

"I do not appreciate being summoned. I sincerely hope you've not invited me here to dish out some mock indignation at what happened. Sometimes mistakes are made in the field. You and your associate know this all too well, given what happened a year ago. Any feelings of remorse which you might attempt to instil inside of me Oliver I will duly mistake for indigestion. If, however, you are here to warn me that your boy has gone off the reservation then I will be grateful and act accordingly. I imagine that Cutter will take great pleasure in tracking him down."

It came as second nature for the senior operative not to admit specifics during conversations which he couldn't be certain were wholly private. Plausible deniability. Yet he felt he got his message across to the fixer – and he had re-established his authority. He ran assets. Assets didn't run him.

"I've not invited you here to give your dog a bone. Rather I'm here to bring his master to heel."

Talbot momentarily sneered, viciously, before relaxing his features and offering up a fake chuckle.

"Ha. How many of those gin and tonics have you had, Oliver? Be careful with your jokes though, as I make it a rule in life to have the last laugh," the CIA agent warned, both darkly and playfully.

"I've not nearly had enough to begin to celebrate with. And I suspect that I'm going to be far more amused by what I have to say that you will be, if you'll permit me the floor for a few minutes," Porter countered, steely and playfully.

"I'll indulge you for a few minutes, Oliver. But I'd take care not to cross any red lines. People who get out of their depth often drown. Watch what you say, old chap."

"I'm always careful to watch what I say, as I know you are, Mason. But in your line of work you have doubtless been asked before, who watches the watchers? I may have cause to apologise to my old Latin master and Juvenal, but "Quis custodiet ipsos custodes?" In answer to the question I watch the watchers, especially when I suspect that they are watching my friends and I. After our initial phone call the other evening I went to bed. Understandably, I had trouble sleeping. I decided to get up again - and contacted several associates of mine. Having mentioned Devlin over the phone I suspected that you had put a team on him. So, I had my team follow yours, the following day."

A flicker of irritation came across Talbot's face but he nodded and forced a smile, indicating that Porter should continue.

"Thankfully, at one point during the observation of their target, your friend sitting over there logged-on to one of your accounts on his computer and gifted the password to us. Using slight variations of the password my associate was subsequently able to hack into several other files and accounts you use. I'm now a veritable font on knowledge, concerning CIA operations conducted on British and European soil during the past ten years. But that information pales in comparison to what the company doesn't know. That you've been a busy but naughty boy - using company money and resources to fund off the books black-ops for personal gain. I've condensed the highlights of your files into the folder on the table, which you can peruse before you leave. Or you may want to glance at it now, so you are fully aware of the unfortunate position you're in. In terms of intelligence, what's mine is yours. Congress would frown on such behaviour. I have friends in the press, on both sides of the pond, who wouldn't be afraid to run the story. Ewan Slater will have more chance of getting elected as

Prime Minister than you will have of becoming a congressman, should I air your dirty laundry in public. Suffice to say I also gained access to one or two of your bank accounts but, as much as I may be a rogue, I'm no common thief. Although I was tempted on more than one occasion to make a donation, in your name, to the charity Alice Pinner has set-up, in honour of her late husband. But, please, before you say something in mock indignation Mason, allow me to continue. I'm about to come to the best bit."

Porter took another sip of his wine and wiped the corner of his mouth with his napkin, to help prolong his guest's ordeal. By now Talbot's face was fixed in a permanent scowl. Beetle-browed. His hands were equally rigid, as they gripped the table like talons.

"Now I must give you some credit, from one devious bastard to another, for your plan. Like Napoleon before Waterloo, you humbugged my Wellington by having Michael take out Pinner instead of Slater. I didn't see it coming. One silhouette looks the same as another. I can understand how you were more confident of us killing Slater than his saintly associate. I would ask that you enlighten me however as to why you wanted to take Pinner off the board. I have a theory, which any silence on your part may speak volumes to. I suspect that you were once Pinner's handler. Either you blackmailed or paid him to provide intelligence, concerning some of his more left-leaning associates. But at some point recently Pinner grew a pair of balls and wanted to be free of you. Or he had heard about your ambitions to run for congress and believed he could blackmail you. If it came out that you were responsible for having funded the man leading the day of protest for when the US embassy opens in Battersea then your political career would fall at the first hurdle. God knows you have made enough enemies, who wouldn't think twice about putting a knife in your back. So, you thought it best to silence Pinner, before he had a chance to talk. It wouldn't be the first asset you've burned. And you decide to sub-contract the job out, so you and the company could evoke plausible deniability should anyone investigate the killing and Pinner's connection to you."

"I'm impressed Oliver. Well played. I'd clap, but I fear that your club has put a ban on any applause or show of emotion," Talbot remarked. Simmering.

"And quite rightly so too."

"Given your resources and smarts I should perhaps try even harder to recruit you now. But I trust you about as much as a Sunni or Shia religious cleric. I forget who is the most untrustworthy and vicious out of the two. It almost changes each day. So how do you propose we move forward? Are you expecting to blackmail me, treat *me* as an asset? You must surely know that, should you attempt to leak anything, you will be signing your own death warrant? Before you embark on a journey of revenge, dig two graves."

"I'm not sure I could consider you to be an asset, in any definition of the term. And revenge is a grubby business. As is blackmail. We're in a position of mutually assured destruction, should we press our respective buttons on each other, so to speak. Should you be tempted to sign my death warrant then you must know I've taken certain steps to make you think twice. You know the drill. I have set up measures whereby if I, or an unknown associate, do not log in a code each day then my files on you will be released to various major news outlets. Should any accident befall me it will trigger instructions – and a payment – made to another associate of mine, who will make sure that you suffer a similar accident. We might be both as trustworthy as Donald Trump or Hilary Clinton – I forget which one is the more untrustworthy out the two, it almost changes each day - but we are also both firm believers in self-preservation. So, do we have an accord?"

Talbot shifted uncomfortably in his chair for a moment and paused, thinking about the ramifications of Porter's words and proposal. But he then nodded his head in agreement, seething as he did so. He gulped down some wine but it couldn't wash away the bitter taste in his mouth. Although in a position of stalemate, the American felt like he had lost. Been outplayed.

"We have an accord, as you pompously say. You must know that I'm not one to forgive and forget though, Oliver."

"You're in good company. Neither am I. Let's be honest, we have no desire to stomach being in one another's presence right now. But I'm happy to for you and your associate to have lunch, on me. Just make sure you leave Maria a handsome tip," Porter said, as he got up from the table.

"As little as you may think of me – and as much as you may have cursed my name over these past weeks - just remember that we have more in common than you would like to admit. Neither of us would make our grandparents' proud. We're both no strangers to grubby business practises. And we have the same blood on our hands."

Talbot removed a piece of fluff from his lapel and adjusted his tie and cufflinks as he spoke, as though if he appeared immaculately groomed his soul would be less tainted.

"I know. But whereas you and your ilk cause problems, Mason, I try to fix them."

Porter made his way off the terrace, although before he left the club he sought out Maria to give her a £50 tip, just in case his guest failed to do so.

18.

Porter was looking forward to getting back home. The Sword of Damocles was no longer hanging over his head. He wanted to see his wife and children again. He would take them out for a meal this evening – and propose a family holiday. No more secrets. No more lies. He could enjoy his retirement again. Breathe freely. Thankfully he had the first-class carriage to himself on the train back to Windsor. He treated himself to reading a few more chapters of Runciman's History of the First Crusade and made some notes for his planned historical novel.

He was also looking forward to giving Devlin the good news. Talbot would just be a bad memory for him now too. He could move forward.

Porter kissed his wife when he got in the door – and hugged her for a few seconds more than normal. He even felt like lifting her up, as if they were characters from a West End musical.

"You're in a good mood. I take it your lunch meeting went well?" Victoria asked, bathing in the rays of her husband's sunny disposition.

"That it did," Porter cheerily replied, resisting the temptation to add that the meeting went well because he would never have to do business with or see his lunch guest ever again.

"Michael Devlin called by the way. I said you were out and would call him back later."

"Did he say anything else?" Porter said, a little surprised and curious, as he had never known Devlin to call the landline before.

"We chatted for a bit. He asked how the children were – and mentioned he would be going away soon and would it be too much trouble if we looked after Violet. I said it'd be fine. I hope that was okay?"

Porter's sunny disposition suddenly became overcast with storm clouds of concern. Devlin hadn't mentioned going away at all to him. Indeed, when he had suggested that his friend go travelling, six months ago, Devlin had assuredly replied, "I've seen enough of the world not to want to see any more of it."

He immediately tried to call his friend. He also left emails and text messages for him to urgently get in touch.

"What's wrong?" Victoria asked, seeing her husband visibly distressed. Porter paced up and down the hallway and his hand trembled as he poured himself a small brandy. Deep furrows lined his brow. His skin seemed to hang off his jaw, like it had turned into melted wax.

"Nothing, I hope. I'm sorry, but I need to head back to London."

"What for?"

"I'm worried about Michael," Porter replied, realising that, for the first time in a long time, he wasn't lying to his wife about the reason he was travelling into town.

"I'll drive you to the station," she immediately resolved, lovingly placing her hands over his in comfort and support. Victoria didn't need to enquire why her husband was worried about not being able to contact his friend. She already knew.

Porter endeavoured to call Devlin multiple times from the train. He even dialled the numbers of his burner phones. But there was no answer. As he got into Paddington and saw the traffic he decided to suffer the underground, as it would take him over an hour to get to Devlin's apartment by car during the rush hour. As he stood up, being buffeted on the District & Circle Line, listening to the inane conversations of his fellow passengers, he started to appreciate why his friend often wore headphones while he was out, to cut him off from the world.

It had been a long day. His lunch with Talbot that afternoon seemed like a lifetime ago. He was bone-tired. Yet Porter still mustered the energy to walk briskly as he alighted from Tower Hill tube station and crossed the bridge, weaving his way through groups of tourists and city workers alike.

As he breathlessly strode over Tower Bridge, in what some might have deemed a mercy dash, Porter took in the Tower of London and remembered how he had taken Victoria there on a date, when they had first started courting. He had read a book on the Tower beforehand, hoping to impress her with his knowledge of the historic building.

Porter cut a desperate figure when he reached Devlin's apartment complex. His tie was askew, he had lost a cufflink on the tube, hair oil and sweat glazed his forehead and his shoes were scuffed. But he didn't much care. He just needed to see Devlin. Put his mind at rest.

He pictured the scene of knocking on his friend's door and waking him up, from a drunken stupor or otherwise. He would recount his meeting with Talbot and take Devlin out to celebrate with a meal and a bottle or two of Sancerre. He thought he might run some ideas by him, regarding his novel. He valued his opinion. He regretted not telling him how much.

Porter's stomach churned – and his legs nearly gave way – as he pictured an alternative scene - of finding his friend dead. His body sprawled across the floor, next to the Sig Sauer pistol. Violet licked his fingers and face trying to wake him up.

Neither scene prevailed when Porter reached Devlin's apartment. But Devlin had committed suicide.

19.

Derek, the grey-haired Pakistani concierge to the building, found the body. Or rather Devlin had arranged for Derek to find the body, after giving instructions, earlier in the morning, for the concierge to pop-up to his apartment at a given time. Devlin had also arranged for a neighbour to dog-sit Violet for the day.

Porter arrived ten minutes or so after Derek had called the emergency services. The concierge sobbed as he spoke and reported what had happened. He was clearly still in shock - and distressed. "He was a good man."

He peered into the room from the doorway. Derek explained that the police had instructed him not to let anyone into the property, until they arrived. And Derek, in his freshly dry-cleaned uniform, was a stickler for the rules.

Life doesn't end with a bang. It ends with a whimper. The air smelled of furniture polish. Devlin had recently cleaned the flat. Death wouldn't be given a chance to fester in the place he and Holly called home. Porter briefly wondered how much Emma had called it home. Devlin lay curled-up, or contorted, on the sofa. He was dressed in a sky-blue shirt and beige trousers. Sunlight flooded the room, almost screechingly so. His pale face resembled polished ivory, or the death mask of a Roman nobleman. Porter couldn't quite decide if he was smiling, or if his mouth was twisted from having suffered a stroke. But Porter told himself his friend was at peace. In some ways, he was happy for him. Devlin's wedding ring glinted in the light, as if winking at Porter. Showing him a sign. A couple of bottles of pills sat on the floor, by the sofa. No doubt Devlin had researched which ones would be most effective. Fail to prepare, prepare to fail. There would have been method in his madness. But how mad had he been? He could still tell a hawk from a handsaw. A framed photo, of Devlin and Holly on their wedding day, lay clutched to his chest. He also noticed a few candles, which looked like votive candles from a church, alight on the window sill.

Porter recalled the last time he and Devlin had spoken. It had been at night, over the phone. Devlin had been drinking and, rarely for him, he opened-up a little to his friend. Porter had mentioned how he didn't want the hitman to go to war with Talbot and Cutter. Devlin replied, "Don't worry. I trust you to fix things, Oliver. The only war that's left is the one with my soul."

Porter couldn't be sure whether, by dying, his friend had won or lost his war. If he had been courageous or cowardly. It was all such a waste.

Music played in the background. As ordered, Derek hadn't touched anything. Not even the volume button on the stereo.

"Now, I've heard of a guy who lived a long time ago
A man full of sorrow and strife
Whenever someone around him died and was dead
He knew how to bring him on back to life
Well, I don't know what kind of language he used
Or if they do that kind of thing anymore
Sometimes I think nobody ever saw me here at all
Except the girl from the Red River shore."

Over the music Porter heard the lamentable sound of Violet moaning from the neighbouring apartment, as if the mongrel already knew something was wrong. He would take the dog home with him.

It's the least I can do.

Later that evening Porter broke down in tears in front of his wife. And quite rightly so too.

The day before he passed away Devlin disposed of the pistol, wiped his computers and removed all other evidence of his profession from his home. He also pre-arranged for his lawyer, Milton Fiennes, to oversee his finances and will. Milton also served as Porter's lawyer. The two men had nicknamed him "Jaggers".

Devlin left his apartment and the bulk of his estate to Emma. She was welcome to keep the capital or sell off his assets and give the money to charities of her choosing. It was up to her. His one stipulation about the house and its contents was that Emma should pass on the framed print of Holbein's *The Ambassadors* – and any books that he wanted from his library – to Oliver.

Certain sums of money were also set aside for John Birch, Terry Gilby and Derek, the concierge, by way of an apology for putting him through the trauma of discovering Devlin's body.

Porter fixed it with Father Matthew so that his friend could have a Catholic funeral. During the service, it was mentioned that Devlin died in his sleep, from heart failure.

More people turned up to the funeral than Porter expected. Neighbours from his apartment block. Regulars from the pub (and a bottle-blonde barmaid who sobbed hysterically; at one-point Porter feared she might even try and drape herself over his coffin). Brothers-in-arms from the regiment, some of whom owed their life to Devlin's bravery and skill in Afghanistan. Porter was pleased that Emma attended the funeral too. He couldn't help but note how she was without her husband.

Porter delivered the eulogy. It was an edited version of one he could have given. He spoke about Devlin's courage as a soldier and how much he loved his foster parents, Bob and Mary Woodward. He also mentioned Holly: "Maybe she called to him in a dream, which is why he didn't want to wake up." Porter didn't share half as much he as could have, but he felt it was enough. Violet would be a prompt for Porter to think about his friend every day.

Just after the service Emma spoke to Porter. She wore an elegant black dress. Her melancholy face was bronzed and blooming with freckles, although she thought it prudent not to wear any make-up lest she wept and looked-like a raccoon from the make-up running.

"I'm not sure if you know but I met Michael for lunch, a couple of weeks before he passed away. I wonder if I should've noticed that something was wrong."

Porter immediately placed a hand on her shoulder and shook his head.

"You shouldn't blame yourself, for anything. Michael was Michael."

He was tempted to make the argument that, if not for her, Devlin would've ended his life sooner. But he thought better of it. Instead Porter recalled a couple of lines from *The Heart of the Matter*. Devlin had bought his friend a first edition of the novel, as a Christmas present.

"No human being can really understand another, and no one can arrange another's happiness."